MISSING GIRLS

MEL SHERRATT

ONE MONTH AGO

He awoke on the settee with a start, his shoulders and back complaining immediately. It hadn't helped that he'd downed almost a full bottle of whisky yesterday. Anything to ease the anger.

He checked his watch: half past eight. He'd been asleep for almost twelve hours, so be it fitfully.

Moving his legs round to the floor, he sat up, waiting for the dull ache behind his eyes to subside. The TV was on low, a news channel showing today's headlines. He wondered how long it would be before his face was plastered all over it.

He stood too quickly, swaying a little, and he held on to the furniture as he made his way to the door.

In the bathroom upstairs, his head throbbed. He stared at himself in the mirror over the sink. There was a hole in the right-hand corner, the cracks coming out from it like a spider's web. He'd done that with his fist just last month. Remembering why wouldn't help him now.

Not bothering to shower, he staggered down the stairs and into the kitchen. The place was a tip even before he'd arrived. Threadbare carpets, curtains that had seen better days. The settee had been covered in a throw to hide its grubbiness. Walls and ceilings were yellow through neglect and smoke damage. But it was the only thing he'd been able to rent without references and a huge deposit.

He shouldn't have come back.

It was raking everything up again. Away from the town and its memories, he could keep everything under control. But now, the darkness was swirling around in his brain, ready to burst out of him. He couldn't stop it. Wouldn't stop it.

While he made black coffee, he stared out of the window. If he closed his eyes, he could picture his sister on the swing, her blonde hair flailing out behind her when she kicked her legs under and then out. She'd be about six, and he would have been thirteen. Her laughter filled his ears as if it were yesterday, as he pushed her higher at her insistence.

The whole family had been lost from the minute she was gone. There had been no one to help them get through their grief. It had been all accusations, dirty looks, fights defending their honour. It had left him in meltdown, and he'd had no choice but to get away.

Yet the pain, the hurt, the unfairness of it all had festered inside him.

He wasn't in the mood for food just yet, so he opened the *Leek News* and spread the paper out on the kitchen table. He turned the pages, reading about families and businesses, accidents, and the deceased. On page nine, he spotted a photo and leaned in closer to view it. His blood ran cold at the sight of the man's face.

It had been twenty years since he'd seen him. He was shaking the hand of a woman in police uniform, both of them smiling at the camera. She was presenting him with a framed certificate.

He scanned the article. Detective Inspector Marsha Clay

was handing out the Business of the Year award for the second year in a row to local garage owner, John Prophet.

He stood up so quickly the chair screeched across the floor. Anger burned inside him again, and he paced the tiny kitchen. How could that be possible? After all this time, Prophet was still getting on with his life, while his sister rotted in a grave. Taken away too soon, robbing her of a future. Ruining his life.

His thoughts became darker still as the hours passed. By the end of the day, he'd made a plan. He was going to do something about the situation himself. It was the only way, and if he played it out quickly, he could be gone before anyone suspected him.

He had to do something. The law had protected the Prophet family for far too long.

Enough was enough.

CHAPTER ONE

Sunday

Marsha Clay pounded through the heather on her way up towards the rocks. If it wasn't so warm, she might not have been out of breath but, despite it only being seven-thirty in the morning, the sun was bright in a clear-blue sky.

Marsha wanted to be there before the crowds descended. The Roaches was a popular tourist spot, with walks ranging from one mile to nearly seven. Yet, coming now, she could almost guarantee that she would share the space with no more than a handful of people.

Ahead, her dog, Larry, charged about as if he hadn't a care in the world. Oh, to be as happy as him, she mused, although as a chocolate Labrador, he looked more like a calf than a march hare prancing up and down.

She reached the top of the rocks and took in a deep breath of fresh air, sighing contentedly afterwards. This was her *Happy Valley*. At its highest point, on clear days, there were views over Staffordshire, Cheshire, and even into Lancashire and Wales.

She sat down on the grass, stretching her legs out in front. Larry came to sit next to her, and she ruffled the dog's fur under his chin. It was so peaceful, the road below quiet for the moment. Definitely somewhere she could clear her head.

She and her husband, Phil, had been arguing again last night. It had started over something simple, and escalated into a mountain of blame, dissatisfaction, and hurt. That morning, she'd left him in bed, needing time on her own to lick her wounds.

How had they come to be living almost separate lives? Nineteen years they'd been married, and at this rate she wasn't sure they would make it to their twentieth anniversary.

Then she scolded herself. At least they *had* lives, which was more than she could say about Dave Harris.

Dave had been sixty-two, and a detective sergeant for the past twenty-seven years. He was five months from retirement when he'd suffered a massive heart attack in the office. Marsha and her team had been there to witness it, all trying desperately to save the man who they'd lovingly called granddad. Devastated when they hadn't been able to.

Dave had never wanted to be anything more than a sergeant. He loved his job and was good at it, teaching Marsha all he knew along the way. It meant for a time, Marsha had gone to a different station to move from detective constable to detective sergeant, but as soon as a vacancy had arrived, she'd returned as a DI.

She and Dave had been a great team. They used to sit in The Old Jug, across from the station after a shift, putting the world to rights. The younger members of the team would rib them about being ancient, even though Marsha was less than a decade older than some. Still, she knew she wouldn't be the police officer she was today without his guidance.

Tomorrow, though, Nathan Clark, who had been acting DS, would be taking over the role permanently, and there would be a new officer in his place. Jess Baxter was transferring from Manchester, where she'd been a DC for over a year. Her story for moving sideways was to be nearer to her mum who lived alone, after the death of her father.

Marsha wasn't ready to welcome a new face, even one as pretty as Jess's. She couldn't contemplate anyone replacing Dave. Every morning, she waited for him to walk in through the door, say something crass, and sit down to stuff his face with his favourite ginger biscuits.

She wiped away a few tears that spilled for her colleague. And then she brushed herself down and stood up. It wasn't often Marsha got a Sunday to do whatever she wanted, and she was going to enjoy every minute of it. Perhaps take the girls out for breakfast if they didn't have anything planned.

She might even ask Phil to join them, if he wasn't working. Phil was a gym instructor, on shifts most weekends, which meant when things were quiet for Marsha, and she wasn't working flat out solving a murder or violent crime, that he was mostly away from the house when she was home. It made for a better atmosphere, she supposed.

'Come on, Larry.' She clipped on his lead. 'Let's go home.'

Ten minutes later, when she arrived back in Leek, all fresh and invigorated from her trip, she found one of her daughters in the kitchen, sitting at the table, a foot up on the seat. She was staring at the screen on her phone.

Larry went straight in for a fuss.

'Hey.' Marsha kissed the top of Cassie's head as she walked past. 'Is your sister home?'

'In the shower,' she replied, not even looking up.

'Dad?'

'Upstairs.'

'Do you fancy breakfast out?'

'I have to be back for twelve as I'm meeting April.'

Marsha laughed inwardly, remembering the times when her girls fitted around what she and Phil were doing rather than the other way round. She glanced at her watch: half past nine.

'I was thinking about going in half an hour. I can drop you off at April's house afterwards, if you like?'

Cassie nodded. 'Okay.'

'Ask Sue if she wants to come with us.'

'Come where?' Sue walked into the kitchen, smiling at the sound of loud thumps coming from Larry as he wagged his tail. She bent down to fuss him, and then he settled in his basket.

'Breakfast out,' Cassie told her. 'Mum's treat.'

'Can you come?' Marsha asked Sue.

'I have a double shift at the pub. I start at twelve.'

'I can get you back in time.' Marsha beamed. 'I'll see if your dad is around.'

'He's working, too. Shift starts at ten.'

Marsha rolled her eyes discreetly. At least Phil had told someone of his plans. She couldn't remember when they'd all gone out together in a long while. What with work, school, and sixth form to fit in around each other, who had time?

She groaned inwardly. She was doing it again, feeling like a work-life balance was impossible, when actually, everyone was doing fine. Weren't they?

'Why don't you message your gran, see if she wants to come, too?' Marsha's mum, Gina, lived in a house further along the road on the opposite side. She'd moved there when Suzanne had been born and had been a godsend, stepping in whenever urgent childcare was needed. Marsha wasn't certain they would have coped without her.

She went upstairs to change, bumping into Phil as he came out of the bathroom. He was dressed in sports gear, dark hair wet from a shower and smelling of something delicious. It almost made her nostalgic. Almost. No matter what, he had a great pair of legs, even better in shorts.

'What time does your shift start?' she asked, although knowing the answer.

'Ten.'

'Can you go in later? I thought you might join us. We're going out for breakfast.'

'Can't, sorry. We're already staff down. I shouldn't even be on the rota.' He avoided her eyes. 'Maybe next weekend?'

Marsha couldn't help feeling deflated, but neither could she complain. Due to the nature of her job, being on call and working long hours when required, she was never able to commit to everything.

Still, a full English breakfast would go a long way towards cheering her up. With at least two mugs of tea.

CHAPTER TWO

Monday

Jess Baxter drew back the curtains to let in the day. Monday morning, and the start of the week beckoned. A new beginning, that was certain.

By the look of the cloudless sky she was faced with, it was going to be another scorcher, so she'd need to dress smart but accordingly. First impressions were important on a day like today.

The garden below had a small lawn and patio area with two chairs and a table, the parasol up from the day before. At the far end was a vegetable patch, next to a greenhouse and a shed. Even without her dad's green fingers, plants were flowering nicely everywhere.

It was much better than her usual view of identical flats opposite her own, and no doubt she'd be seeing something similar soon.

Turning back to her childhood bedroom, she sighed. She missed her apartment already. It had been in a new block with all mod cons, ten minutes' walking distance from the Northern Quarter, with its pubs and wine bars, cafés, and restaurants. Drinks out with friends; celebratory meals for birthdays. It was fifteen minutes' drive into the police station, traffic willing, and in an area that she felt adequately safe in. Yet, she'd had to leave it all behind.

Half an hour later and almost ready, she was applying her lipstick when there was a knock on the door. Her mum, Pam, walked in.

'Jess, it's time to get... oh, you're already up.'

'Of course I am. My alarm went off an hour ago. I start at eight.'

'Sorry, love. I didn't want you to be late on your first day.'

Jess held back her sigh and smiled instead. 'I've been getting myself up since I left home. I'm sure I'll be able to manage it now, too.'

Pam's face dropped. With Jess being an only child, her mum had always mollycoddled her at every chance. Now that her dad was gone, Jess could see her obsessive, caring, and fussing routine being thrust onto her instead. It was one of the reasons why she'd left home so early.

Jess had been back five days. It was a temporary measure, until she could get fixed up with somewhere closer to her new base. Even so, Pam had redecorated, making everything fresh for her.

'You know I worry about you,' Pam went on. 'I can't help it, with your job being so dangerous these days.'

'I know, and I love you for it.'

'Why you couldn't have a job in an office, or somewhere with regular hours, is beyond me.'

Oh, now she was getting the folded-arms pose.

'It wouldn't be half as much fun,' she teased.

'It would be better for my heart.'

Jess rested a hand on her mum's cheek and smiled, trying

not to notice the years creeping by. For the best part, they had been kind.

Pam kept herself slim and fit, and, to her knowledge, was healthy. They were similar in looks with short hair and small builds. Pam had glasses, Jess wore contact lenses. Each one had a stubborn streak that meant they often fought for the last word.

'I'm going to be late if I don't leave now.' Jess reached for her bag and popped her phone in it.

'But I've made breakfast,' Pam protested. 'I thought we could eat together.'

'Sorry, Mum. New boss wants me in early.' *Thankfully.* 'I'll grab something at the canteen.'

A few minutes later, Jess turned left onto the A523, taking her to Leek, and was soon enjoying the familiarity of the sharp bends and corners on a road she'd driven along for many years before moving to Manchester.

Although a main road, the land around it wasn't built up. Farms were scattered around, with large stretches of fields, and then a row of houses would appear until the greenery was back.

If anything, Jess would enjoy this run the most about being back in Rushton Spencer. Much better than sitting in bumper-to-bumper traffic to travel a few miles.

It took fifteen minutes to get to Leek, and she felt a huge sense of pride when she indicated to turn into the town's police station. She'd paid it a flying visit yesterday to check everything out, bringing Pam out for Sunday lunch at The Duck Goose Bistro a couple of streets away.

Jess showed her warrant card to get through the security gates and parked at the rear of the building. Glancing upwards as she locked her car, she noted a rectangular building set over three floors. Sunlight streamed into windows travelling from one end to the other at waist level, no doubt ensuring the need for blinds to be drawn to shield the glare of the sun.

A line of liveried cars were parked to her left, next to a skip that was almost full of plasterboards and pieces of wood. At her interview, her new line manager had mentioned that a few rooms downstairs were being refurbished after a long wait to get the necessary funding.

The place was tiny in comparison to where she'd worked before. It was going to take some adjusting to life away from a big city, but she was up for the challenge, and looking forward to it. Once she'd settled in and met everyone, and her nerves had abated, things would be fine. Besides, she needed to be somewhere she would feel safe.

She went round to the front of the building, having been told to go through the public reception area until she had her access passes.

The man on the main desk seemed to be mid-thirties, tall with dark spiked hair. A fan was whirring away on his desk, paperwork fluttering in the breeze it created, held down by a Superman mug. His tie was discarded on the desk behind him, the top two buttons on his shirt undone.

Jess herself was dressed in a navy skirt suit, her jacket over her arm, and an orange sleeveless blouse. She'd thought of shrugging the jacket on for first appearances, but the heat was stifling, and it seemed excessive.

'Hi.' She smiled. 'DC Baxter. It's my first day. I need to ask for Marsha Clay.'

'Well, hello, DC Baxter. Welcome to the jungle.'

'Call me Jess.'

'Call me Ben. Pleased to meet you. I'll need your scribble in the book beside you, and then if you take a seat, I'll give Marsha a bell.'

'Thanks.' A nice attitude as well as a smile to match her own, she mused.

To her left was a row of metal seating attached to the floor. She didn't want to sit down so she pretended to study the noticeboard.

A domestic abuse flyer fought for room next to a poster about taking care of your vehicle. There was a photo of a small child, warnings of the danger of leaving youngsters in a hot car, and details of a meeting next week with the local councillor.

'Marsha will meet you on floor one,' Ben said, pointing right. 'I'll buzz you through.'

'Thanks, again. Nice to meet you.'

'Likewise. Good luck.'

Jess pushed on the door, finding stairs and a lift ahead. She decided on the stairs, smiling her appreciation at two uniformed officers who made way for her to pass before continuing on their way.

On the small landing in between floors, she glanced at the passing view, only able to see a brick wall and the corner of a graveyard. Not exactly welcoming, she laughed inwardly.

CHAPTER THREE

The traffic was heavy as he turned onto High-Up Lane, leading on to Meerbrook Road, but it thinned out quite quickly. The area ahead was well known to him now, after familiarising himself with the layout around the farm for four weeks.

He'd sat for an hour at a time, watching how many vehicles came past, trying not to stand out too much.

Discreetly, he hoped, he'd got to know the regulars who were probably residents nearby, what day of the week the bin men came, and how irregular delivery drivers arrived.

Having finally decided that the best time to strike would be around nine o'clock in the morning, when a lot of people would be out at work, or perhaps dropping kids off at school, he'd made ample plans to get there with plenty of time to spare.

The weather was hot again. Already he could feel sweat forming on his brow. But that might have something to do with his nerves.

Yet he hadn't had to talk himself into action that morning. He'd woken up early, booze-free, clear about his intentions. He was going to send out a message that he wouldn't let them get away with it anymore. One that would get everyone listening.

After driving half a mile, he parked the car in the small lay-by, created for residents' parking but often used as a place to pull in so that other vehicles could pass. He wound his side window down and listened.

No one stirred in the houses across from him, a row of identical compact terraced cottages that, to him, all had individual looks. Except for birdsong, it was almost silent. In the distance, the rumble of a tractor could be heard, and the faint whine of the traffic.

Not wanting to draw attention to himself, he started the engine and set off on the few metres to Dairy Croft Farm. He drove slowly, hoping not to alert anyone inside the property, bumping over the cattle grid.

The house came into view, and he rounded the bend in the drive. It was larger than he'd thought after only seeing it from afar.

Anger ripped through him – or was it envy? How did Prophet live like this, while he had to rent that poxy house, doing a grim job, not a career in sight?

Prophet should be in prison after what he'd done. He didn't deserve any happiness.

He passed several outbuildings before he was at the property. There was no one in sight, so he pulled in at the side of a large barn to his right.

He planned to do the job quickly. Having the element of surprise would be the best action. Even so, he got out of the vehicle, leaving the keys in the ignition and the door open for a quick getaway.

At least there wasn't noisy gravel underfoot as he crossed the circular turn-around point in front of a large entrance. He walked slowly over the block paving, savouring the moment that was coming up.

In a few seconds, Prophet's life would be over. His would, too, but he wasn't concerned with that. All he wanted was revenge. And after all this time, it would be good to get even at last.

The silence around him now seemed surreal, a little eerie. Everywhere he'd lived had been full of noisy neighbours, with no thoughts for anyone else's wellbeing. Dirty properties, scally tenants. He'd never owned a property, not even when he'd been married briefly.

And all that time, John Prophet had lived here, or somewhere similar in stature. How could that be right, after what he'd done? Twenty years ago, he'd ruined their family, and now it was his time to pay.

He reached the door and stood in front of it, not moving for a moment. He took a deep breath in as he relished what was to come.

Then he knocked.

CHAPTER FOUR

Jess saw a woman with shoulder-length blonde hair waiting at the top of the stairs. She was medium height, thin and dressed casually in cropped trousers, tan loafers, and a white short-sleeved blouse with a granddad collar. Her full-lipped smile seemed sincere, blue eyes enhanced with make-up, welcoming. Around her neck was a chain with a tiny silver skull.

'Hello again, Jess.' Marsha smiled and offered a hand. 'Nice to have you on board.'

'Hello, ma'am.' Jess shook it, noticing a tattoo on her inner arm. It was a row of words that she hadn't got time to read without appearing nosy. 'Thanks, I'm looking forward to settling in.'

'Boss will do, or Marsha. Guv at a push, but not ma'am. It makes me sound like a queen, even though some of my team are sure I'm a diva.' She rolled her eyes and then smiled to show there was no malice.

Jess had met her new DI a month earlier when she'd been interviewed for the role. She'd told no one what had been happening in Manchester, instead asking for a transfer when things had got to the point where they were making her ill, and then citing her mum being on her own as an excuse. She already felt better knowing she wouldn't bump into *him* during her working day anymore.

'Thanks for coming in so early.' Marsha pushed her ID card up close to a keypad and opened a door. 'I'll do housekeeping first, and by then the team should be in.'

They walked along a corridor with Wedgwood-blue carpet and beige walls.

'Toilets, to the right. Kitchen to the left. You'll find the incident room at the bottom.' Marsha waved a hand at each as she went past. 'The press room is downstairs, and the higher-ranking officers are up one floor – aren't they always? As is the canteen – someone got their planning wrong there, methinks. Having said that, the food is pretty decent, but if you fancy nipping out, there are numerous tea and coffee shops in the town.'

She pointed to the window where Jess could just about glimpse a tiny corner of the market square, its cobblestones mostly covered by parked vehicles.

'Next room along is where you'll find the DCI, and this is us – the Major Crimes Team.' Marsha went through another door and gave a twirl, her arms outstretched. 'Voila! That's all there is to it. Sorry it's nothing like GMP. I bet you're used to all mod cons – glass partitions, lots of windows, airy spaces. Not a sniff of damp in the air.'

Jess smiled to show she didn't mind.

Marsha nodded her head towards a bank of four desks in the middle. 'You're at the far right. It's a great spot. I much prefer my back to a wall than a door.' She threw a thumb over her shoulder. 'I'm in the cupboard, I mean office, although my door mainly stays open. It gets a little cosy, but we're a close team.

'In between major cases, we have rural thefts to deal with,

as well as burglaries in town to keep us busy, plus we like to get ourselves known in the community, hence we do a lot of school and safety visits. We're all Leek born and bred, and I'm sure everyone will help you with anything you need to know.'

'I was sorry to hear about Dave Harris,' Jess said, wanting to address the elephant in the room straight away. 'I believe he'd worked here a long time?'

'Since he was eighteen.' Marsha reached for a photo. 'That's him, there. He was a gentle soul, firm when required, but always fair. I miss him.'

Jess peered at the image. A man in his sixties was sitting at the desk next to the one she'd been allocated, a mug of tea in one hand and a biscuit in the other. His smile was friendly, happy.

'He looked like a jolly soul,' Jess said.

'He was indeed.' Marsha gave a sigh and moved on to a door at the back.

'This is the store cupboard. Coats and stab vests, hi-vis jackets, etcetera are stored in there.' She glanced down at Jess's feet. 'You'll need to buy wellies if you don't have some. Even in summer, we can get torrential downpours that leave us having to traipse through muddy fields.'

'They're in the boot of my car.'

'Great!' Marsha grinned. 'Well, I think that's it for now. The gang will be in shortly. Your ID pass is in your in-tray, along with your passwords. I'll leave you to familiarise yourself with everything in time, and for now, you'll be shadowing me this week. I thought I'd show you around your new patch. You'll know some of it, I'm sure?'

'Vaguely, yes. I've had many a good night out in the town itself.'

'Ah, student nights?'

Jess nodded. 'Lots of good memories.'

'Why did you choose Manchester?'

'A bigger division, that's all. I got a flat share there as soon as I could, save me commuting.'

'And now you're working in a town rather than a city, with a smaller team. I'm sure there's a story there about why and that you'll tell me in time.'

Jess blushed. And there was her thinking her tale about keeping her mum company had worked.

'But first things first,' Marsha went on. 'Tea or coffee?'

'Coffee, please. No sugar and a spot of milk.' Jess reached into her bag to retrieve her purse. 'How much do I owe for the tea club?'

'First week is free. After that, it's three quid. We have a fortnightly rota for fetching supplies. I'll pop your name down in Dave's place.'

While Marsha went to make a brew, Jess took a minute to glance around her new surroundings. The office was the smallest she'd worked in so far, yet the windows let in more natural light than she'd expected.

Underneath them was a row of filing cabinets, several boxes of A4 paper on their tops, and to her right was a whiteboard, split with a line of black tape, where timelines would be established, she assumed. Jess saw a digital screen, too.

Next to them was a large green pinboard, marks all over it, and a small table with a pot of pens, a board rubber, and a white teddy bear sporting a red T-shirt.

Feeling conspicuous even though alone, she sat on the chair and lowered its height to make it suitable. Idly, she pulled out a drawer to see pens, a desk tidy, and a bright blue stress ball.

Except for a computer, phone, and in-tray, the desk itself was bare. Later in the week, she'd bring in some personal items, but for now she wanted to settle in. It all felt alien but, no doubt by the end of the week, it would seem like she'd worked there for ages.

She was also curious to see who'd be sitting at the desks around her.

CHAPTER FIVE

Despite her misgivings the day before, Marsha had a feeling that Jess was going to fit in well. She'd had glowing references from her DCI in Greater Manchester Police, and she'd come across really well in her interview. Personable, likeable, although not too full of herself.

Still, Marsha would worry for a while until she got to know Jess better. It was one thing to smile and answer the correct questions at an interview. It was another not to alter the dynamics of a team too much, one that had bonded for years, decades when it came to her and Dave Harris.

Overthinking was Marsha's bugbear. Even as a detective inspector, she couldn't switch off the feeling that she wasn't good enough. That she shouldn't be doing the job. That her future was bleak. That her life was running away with her, and she hadn't been successful.

Yet, she had achieved so much, and all before she was forty next year. As well as her career, she and Phil had raised two daughters. If she said so herself, they'd made a pretty good job of that.

Obviously, she kept all her maudlin thoughts to herself. It wouldn't do to seem vulnerable.

Perched on the end of a desk, a mug in hand, she was chatting to Jess, hoping to put the young woman at ease. It was hard to transfer, leaving behind people you saw more than your family at times. She'd had to do it once herself, and it had taken her an age to gel with her new crowd. There had been a couple of detective constables who'd had their noses pushed out of joint after she'd got the job they'd both coveted.

'I think you'll be—' The door opened before she had time to finish, and two men and a woman walked in the office together.

'You lot are like buses,' Marsha joked.

'Well, someone has to get Nathan out of bed,' the younger of the men chided. 'He's getting so old now.'

'Speak for yourself, babyface.' Nathan pushed Connor as he was about to sit at his desk. He almost fell to the floor when the chair moved but righted himself at the last second.

'Eejit,' Connor cried.

'All right, you two.' Marsha put down her mug and thrust out her hand. 'Lady and gents, meet the newest member of the team, Jess Baxter. As you know, she's transferred from Manchester into the wilds of the Staffordshire Moorlands.'

Teasing comments drifted across to Jess, who grinned at them manically whilst waving.

'This is DS Nathan Clark.' Marsha pointed to the man who was settling into the desk beside them. 'On the beat for six years, been a detective for four. Don't let him fool you into thinking he's a dead ringer for a young Tom Cruise.'

Next she turned to the joker, on the desk opposite Nathan.

'That's Connor Wilson. He's been working here since he

joined the force at eighteen, eight years in uniform and two years as a DC.'

'Pleased to meet you,' Jess replied.

Marsha went round the room to where a young woman with blonde wavy hair and the bluest of eyes was now sitting across from her.

'And this one here is my lovely Emma Bedford.'

'That's favouritism right there,' Nathan commented.

Marsha ignored him, placing her hands on Emma's shoulders. 'Emma is an information officer and has been with us for five years. She came as a replacement for a DC but, in my opinion, turned out to be just as valuable. She looks after the office, retrieves information and intel for us, and does a lot of the legwork that cracks our cases. And she never moans about menial tasks, unlike some I can mention.' She glared at Connor.

'Me?' Connor pretended to be wounded, pressing a hand to his chest. 'I never shirk anything.'

'Getting tea and coffee when it's your week.' Marsha used her hands to count on. 'You're never around when sandwiches need fetching, and always the last one at the bar in the pub. Need I go on?'

'Nope.' Connor grinned. 'But what about you, boss?' Does Jess know what she's letting herself in for, working with you?'

'Cheeky. I joined at twenty-four, was a PC for six years, a detective constable for four, then a sergeant for three. For the past two years I've been an inspector, and I bloody love my job.'

'She has to say that because it's your first day,' Emma teased.

'Joking aside.' Marsha looked at them all in turn. 'I know we've had a rough few months, and Nathan has done a great job of filling some tough boots, so I want you to welcome Jess with open arms. I trust you three to show her the ropes and help her with whatever she needs. You got that?'

'Yes, boss,' went around the room.

Marsha's phone rang in her office, and she marched off. 'Good. Now whose turn is it to make a brew?'

'I bet she's only just finished one,' Connor said.

'I heard that!'

While Marsha took the call, Jess got to her feet. 'I think I should make drinks, so I can put a face to the mug at least.'

'That's a bit cheeky.' Connor chuckled. 'I'm no mug.'

'That's a matter of opinion,' Emma said.

Laughter burst from them.

Marsha clicked her fingers for silence, and they waited for her to come off the phone.

'We've had a call from Control,' she said. 'One male deceased, one female unconscious, although we assume she might have raised the alarm before that. No one spoke on the emergency line. The front door was open when uniformed officers arrived. Not sure if it's a domestic until we get there. Jess, you come with me. Everyone else in a pool vehicle. Meerbrook Road. Dairy Croft Farm.'

They rushed down the stairs and out to the car park. Jess climbed into the passenger seat of Marsha's black Audi. Blues and twos were activated, and soon they were out of the station and into passing traffic that had slowed for them.

'Meerbrook Road is off High-Up Lane,' Marsha explained. 'It's just over two miles out of town.'

'I passed that on my way in. Never driven up there, though. What's it like?'

'A few farms, rows of picturesque cottages, that kind of thing. Usually quiet, but then again, isn't everywhere until this kind of thing happens on your doorstep?'

Jess held on as Marsha floored the vehicle with expertise. Then, almost as quickly, she slowed down, indicated right, and turned into the lane. They drove for a minute or so, until the properties thinned out, replaced by low stone walls and fields either side.

'Can you watch out for a sign?' Marsha asked. 'There are farms off the beaten track up here. I don't want to drive past it.'

'Up ahead.' Jess pointed to where she could see the blue lights on a marked car flashing.

They rounded a corner, and Marsha pulled into the farm, slowing down to bump over a cattle grid. 'Hold on.'

Jess did as she was told. 'I was hoping to have had a little time to get to know the crew before my first case.'

'Well, as every police officer knows,' Marsha said, 'crime never waits for anyone.'

CHAPTER SIX

Lucy Prophet climbed into the car, popped on her sunglasses, cranked the music up, and activated the electronic gates to let herself out of the property.

Once on the main road, she settled back, letting out a sigh of contentment. She'd enjoyed the last hour immensely. At least something had put a smile on her face that morning, to make up for a lousy couple of days.

She and her husband, Dan, had been arguing for most of the weekend. It had started on Saturday afternoon when she'd rung him at work to see what time he'd be home. The garage closed at midday, but he said he had work to catch up on and could do it better when he was alone.

Lucy had suggested he should bring it home, sit in the garden because the weather was nice, and do it with a bottle of something cold to share. But Dan had said the kids would distract him, and he'd never get anything done if he drank a glass of wine or two.

She'd snapped at him then, about putting the business first: he'd argued back that without it they wouldn't be where they were today.

Lucy knew he was right, yet she also wanted to feel as if she was married. It was like being a single parent most days, and yet, she worked part-time at the garage and was never given credit for it.

Dan was running the show now his father has finally retired. He'd always worked long hours – wasn't that half of the problem – so the majority of childcare came to her. Lucy had been full-time until she'd had the girls and become a stay-at-home mum. Now, keeping her hand in with the business gave her the best of both worlds.

Sunday hadn't been much better, but at least they'd had last night by themselves. Yesterday, they'd been out to lunch with Dan's parents, and then the girls had stayed overnight with them.

But there had been an atmosphere between Dan and his father again. It was getting more noticeable to her. Sylvia, Dan's mother, didn't seem concerned about it. She'd been her usual self, rolling her eyes at Lucy when the men started bickering.

Even before the weekend, she and Dan had been going through a rough patch for a while. But there were Tamara and Maisie to consider if they went their separate ways. She didn't want to think about that, not yet anyway.

She hummed, casting a glance over the sky. It was going to be another glorious day. She smiled to herself, remembering how annoyed she'd been that a teacher training day had been latched on to the weekend. The timing couldn't be more perfect now. She was looking forward to a day in the garden, with the girls in and out of their inflatable pool.

She stopped at traffic lights, the usual morning rush hour at its heaviest. While she was stationary, she made a mental list of the things she wanted to call for on the way back. The butcher's was the first stop – she needed fresh meat for the impromptu barbecue she'd decided to have that evening, and more wine, too. Perhaps a nice dessert. There was never a reason not to have cake.

Children from the local high school were hogging the pavement as they went past in their white short-sleeved shirts and burgundy ties, dark trousers, or short skirts, grouped in twos and threes.

Lucy laughed at the drama of some of their expressions; the boys showing off, the girls on their phones with their besties alongside. Giggling, shouting, pushing, no doubt a lot of cussing. At least some of the schools were in today, she sighed. Still, a day off with Tamara and Maisie wasn't a hardship.

Finally through Leek, she drove on the main road to Macclesfield. A few minutes later, she turned into High-Up Lane. The noise was left behind with every metre she travelled, but, when she rounded a corner about half a mile later, her hand tapping on the steering wheel, she slowed.

There were police vehicles ahead, one blocking the road. A man and a woman she recognised from the local pub were standing at their front gate, observing developments.

An officer walked towards her, and she pressed the button for the window to go down.

'You can't come this way, ma'am,' he said. 'There's been a police incident, and the road is closed for the foreseeable future.'

'I only need to go another few hundred metres. Can I leave my vehicle here and walk?'

'Sorry, no one is allowed to go further than the cordon.'

Lucy sighed. It would take her a good half hour to go back to the main road, drive up through the lanes and drop down to the farm. She popped the car into reverse, but then a thought gripped her, and she paled.

'Excuse me, Officer,' she stopped him. 'The incident – it isn't at Dairy Croft Farm, is it?'

The officer's friendly expression changed, telling her all she needed to know.

She switched off the engine and got out of the car. 'I have to find out what's going on. My family lives there. Why won't you tell me anything?'

'Ma'am, let me make a call and see what I can do.'

As he walked off to get a bit of privacy, she almost followed him. Then she reached for her phone and dialled Dan's number.

'Where are you?' she said as soon as he answered.

'I'm just coming down Solomon's Hollow – why?'

'Something is going on at your parents' home. There're police everywhere, and the road is closed and—'

'What do you mean? Can you see the house?'

'No, I can't get close enough.' She took her voice down a notch or two, trying to stay calm. Dan was driving. It wasn't fair to worry him too much.

But then panic took over again, and she let out a sob. 'They won't let me near. Something bad has happened. It's all cordoned off.'

'Hang on, let me pull over.'

She waited, hearing his indicator and then the engine stopping.

'Why won't they let you through?' he asked.

'I don't know, and I can't see what's happening from here. What's going on, Dan? Why are the police here?'

'I'll come to you. I'll be as quick as I can, I'm only half an hour away at the most.'

Lucy disconnected the call and waited for the officer to return. A car parked behind her, the driver peeping his horn.

'You're in my way!' he shouted.

'You can't get through, so there's no point having a go at me,' she snapped. 'The police have blocked the road for an incident.'

'What kind of an incident?'

'I don't know! That's what I'm waiting to find out.'

He muttered something incomprehensible and slammed his car into reverse.

She moved to the side of the road, leaning against the wall to steady herself, praying nothing had happened to her family.

CHAPTER SEVEN

Marsha drove along the driveway, which was more of a dirt track with a picket fence either side of two fields.

Below, down a bank, she could see two patrol cars and an ambulance parked in an arc in front of an impressive stone farmhouse. Several outbuildings stood in a line to their right, alongside a new oak build with two vehicles inside it.

An officer in uniform approached them as soon as she came to a stop.

'Were you first on scene, Seb?' Marsha asked, introducing him to Jess as PC Hadley.

'Yes, boss. Me and Becky.' He threw a thumb over his shoulder, indicating his colleague who was standing by the front door. 'One male in his sixties deceased, several stab wounds, found in the hall. One female the same age, unconscious, nasty wound to the head. She's in the back of the ambulance. They'll be moving her to the hospital shortly.'

'Right, thanks.' Marsha pulled a clipboard and a roll of crime scene tape from the boot of the car. 'Can you do the honours? Get someone to secure the area around the gates at the top as well as here, and then note down anyone who comes and goes, please.'

'Will do.' Seb nodded and left them to it.

Nathan and Connor joined them, and Marsha handed out forensic suits.

'Nathan, Connor, take a gander outside and tell me what you see. Jess, you're with me.'

They dressed quickly in protective gear, Marsha's eyes flitting everywhere, taking in the surroundings. The farmhouse was bordered by fields, which meant it would be easy for anyone to reach the property almost unseen.

She kept her thoughts to herself as they split up to do their various tasks. At the front door, Marsha recognised PC Becky Stroud and stopped to talk to her before going inside.

'Jess, Becky. Becky, Jess. Has there been any change since you first arrived?'

'No, ma'am.' Becky pointed to the door. 'I pulled that to so it's not such a shock when you go in. He's on the floor right behind.'

Marsha had known Becky as long as Seb. They'd both been based at the station for some years now. That was the thing with living in a market town with only two high schools and one college. Everyone knew everyone else, so it was inevitable the local officers who turned up to help, or, like Becky and Seb, who were first on scene, were almost always known to her.

Marsha nodded and stepped through the front door, followed by Jess. She almost stopped when she saw their victim. He was lying on his back, blood soaked through the pale-green T-shirt and down the front of his shorts. His right arm was outstretched, blue eyes open wide, pain clear to all who looked in them. Marsha spotted five stab wounds to his chest and abdomen; reckoned there were as many defence wounds on his arms.

'I know him,' she said quietly to Jess. 'His name is John Prophet. I only saw him last month. He owns a garage, just off Buxton Road.'

Marsha glanced behind him to see blood on the carpet, as if someone had been dragged. The table in the hall had gone on its side, a phone covered in bloody fingerprints on the carpet, and a handprint on the bottom of the wall.

'This is where we found the female,' Becky said.

'I think she was attacked here, too, and then dragged herself to get the phone to raise the alarm. Maybe the suspect wanted to kill the male and the female tried to stop him.' Marsha pursed her lips. 'Is the rest of the house empty?'

'We did a quick sweep of it, didn't see anything out of the ordinary.'

'Okay. If you can guard the door, thanks.'

They went through to the kitchen. Marsha glanced around, taking in everything. It had a country-style feel to it, with an Aga, a double Belfast sink, multi-coloured tiles above rows of cream units. A red Smeg fridge had a child's drawing attached to it with a magnet.

The breakfast dishes were still out on the large pine table. Marsha noted they seemed to have been disturbed as they were eating. Half-drunk mugs of tea stood next to partially empty cereal bowls. Toast on separate plates. A pot of homemade jam with its lid off, a knife with remnants of it by its side.

Something wasn't right.

'This table is set for four people.' Marsha pointed to it. 'We need to check the rooms again, make sure no one is hiding.'

'So it's not a domestic?' Jess queried.

'It's unlikely, unless someone known to them is responsible.'

'You said you know him. Does he have family?'

'They have a son, Dan. Married with two children. I know him, too. He's going to be devastated, if he isn't involved.'

'Do you think he will be?'

Marsha pouted. 'It's always possible. But someone could have harmed them and then left.' Marsha put a hand to the kettle. The water was lukewarm. 'How does one person end up dead, one injured, and yet with no signs of anyone else? How many vehicles are parked outside? I saw two coming in.'

Jess moved to the window. 'Yes, a Golf and a Toyota Hilux. I can't see anything else.'

'Let's leave the house now and wait for the forensics team. There's nothing more we can do at the moment.'

In the hallway again, Marsha went down on her haunches next to the body of John Prophet. It was always more of a shock when she knew the victim. It seemed personal, somehow, and yet with a population of twenty thousand in the town, it was bound to happen.

'Who did this to you?' she spoke quietly.

Close to, she could see the attack had been brutal. She reckoned he wouldn't have had time to react. Maybe his arm was out to his side as he saw his wife for the last time. Did he expect her to die, too? She shuddered at the thought.

'Boss?'

Marsha looked up to see Connor coming towards her. 'There's a woman arrived at the top gate. She says the couple are her in laws.'

'Don't let her anywhere near the crime scene. We can't let her see what's—'

'She's asking about her children, two girls, eight and four. They were staying overnight, and she's here to collect them.'

'Ah, no.' Marsha's blood ran cold. She hated being right.

After calling it in, she went outside to the ambulance. A paramedic was closing the doors, another had started the engine.

'Wait!' Marsha urged.

'No time, sorry. We need to move her.'

'She hasn't regained consciousness?'

'Not yet, I'm afraid.'

Marsha grimaced at the news. Along with the missing children, this was going to be one tough case for her emotionally.

Right now, though, she had to focus on the job in hand. She needed to talk to the daughter-in-law.

CHAPTER EIGHT

Marsha and Jess removed their forensic paraphernalia and popped them into evidence bags. The forensic team were arriving so, after brief introductions, they walked up to the main gate to speak to the woman whose children she believed were missing.

Although they hadn't had time to chat, Marsha was keen to see how Jess would fit in. First she wanted to know how she reacted around families of the deceased. It was always a challenging time, particularly where children were concerned.

'Have you been involved in many missing children cases?' she asked.

'Several where the kids have turned up. One deceased child, killed by his older brother who hid his body in nearby woods.'

'So what would you do first on this case?'

'Get as much detail as possible from the parents, about the grandparents as well as the children. Set up house-to-house and a search team in the vicinity. Get local press to spread the message, but make sure they don't become too intrusive. Then check with financial forensics, and liaise with social services to see if the children are known to them. Then I'd start a timeline of the victim's last few days.'

'Good.'

They approached the gates to see a press van already there.

'Speak of the devil. Bloody vultures,' Marsha muttered. 'We have a crime reporter for the *Leek News*. He's not too bad, but this rabble must be from further afield as I don't recognise any of them. How did they hear about it already?'

'Beats me, but you know what they say. News travels fast.'

Marsha took out her phone. 'I'll get Nathan to move them back. We don't want them seeing anything we're about to do.'

A woman who looked to be in her late thirties was standing with Seb. Although she was dressed in T-shirt and shorts, she was hugging herself. Her hair was tied back in a ponytail, tears making tramlines down her make-up. When she saw Marsha and Jess, she moved forward.

'Have you got them?' she shouted. 'Please, I have to know.'

'Let her through,' Marsha told Seb. 'I'll get her details.' She beckoned the woman forward. 'Come with me, please. It's Lucy, isn't it?'

'Yes. Where are they?' The woman ran towards them.

'Let's talk in my car. It's not ideal, but we can't go into the house.'

'What do you mean?'

'It's a crime scene.' Marsha pointed to her vehicle.

'Why, what's happened?'

Marsha said nothing until she was in the car. The woman scrambled into the passenger seat. Jess slid in the back and took out her notebook.

'John and Sylvia are your in-laws, isn't that right?' Marsha spoke calmly.

'Yes. Please, are they okay?'

'I'm afraid not. Although there will need to be formal identification, there is a deceased male in the property who we believe to be John Prophet, and a female who has been taken to hospital with head injuries. We believe that's Sylvia. I'm so sorry.'

Lucy gave out a wail. 'My girls, where are they? Can you take me to them?'

'Lucy, there are signs that four people were at the breakfast table, but we found no one else in the house.'

The cry was guttural this time.

Marsha glanced at Jess surreptitiously. It wasn't the best of places to tell anyone bad news, but they couldn't let Lucy into the property, so it had to be done that way.

'You say you have two daughters?' she went on.

'Tamara and Maisie. Tamara is eight and Maisie four. Someone has taken them, haven't they?'

'We can't be certain at this moment,' Marsha soothed. 'There are officers searching every inch of the house and grounds. They could be hiding if they're frightened. If so, do you have any idea where they might be? Do the girls play hide and seek with their grandparents?'

Lucy thought for a moment and then shook her head. 'I'm sorry, I can't think of anywhere they might be. I have to go and find them.' She reached for the door handle.

Marsha placed a hand on her arm. 'That's not a good idea. We need to keep the crime scene as sterile as possible until we know more about what happened.'

'But you can't—'

'Have you rung Dan?'

'Yes, he was on his way back from Buxton. He'll be about ten minutes now.'

'Can you show me any recent photos of your girls?' Even though it was vital she got the images shared as soon as possible, Marsha thought this would take Lucy's mind off things.

Maybe by the time they'd done that, Dan would arrive to comfort her.

And then she'd have to get them both away from the scene as soon as possible. Everything was on display. Stepping into the house for the first time after the crime scene had been cleared was going to be traumatic enough. She didn't want them to have memories of police vehicles and officers all over the place.

Lucy got out her phone and scrolled until she came to one. 'This was taken yesterday.'

Marsha took the phone from her. Two beautiful girls stared back from the screen. Tamara was in the background, two fingers held up in a victory sign, and the image of her mother. The younger child, Maisie, was growing into the role, too. Both had long brown hair with lots of brightly coloured clips, and shining eyes full of laughter. Marsha could tell they were happy and well balanced.

'May I use this, please?' she asked. 'We'll need something to circulate to the press, and I think this is a wonderful picture to share.' She didn't say it would tug at people's heartstrings, the way it had with her own.

Lucy nodded.

A vehicle screeching to a halt had them turning their heads. All three women glanced up to see a man running to Seb.

'Dan!' Lucy burst into tears again.

'Wait here,' Marsha told her. 'I'll go to him.'

As she got out of the car, she wondered how she was going to play this. Lucy and Dan were in full view of the press, yet they would want to hug each other, share their grief. But she had to let them see one another.

There was a large barn at the side. Perhaps they could use that. It wasn't ideal, in fact, it was pretty crap really. But they needed their privacy.

'Take Lucy into the barn, and I'll bring Dan to you,' she told Jess.

Jess nodded.

By now, a crowd was gathering at the side of the main gate. Marsha surmised it was the neighbours, as they were there so quickly. Still, she took a look at each one.

There had been two occasions during her career where their suspect had watched on as the person they had murdered was taken away, the crime scene worked. One had even been involved in the search for the victim. People were weird. Personally, she never understood how it would be a thrill.

She braced herself and ushered Dan through. He was the same age as her, with a full head of hair and tanned skin. She could still remember the time that he'd been out with a friend and asked her for a date. Luckily for both of them, she never wanted to meet, but they had remained good friends after leaving school. They had a lot of respect for each other.

His face was etched with worry, and she swallowed. She didn't want to cause him any further pain but knew, no matter what she said, it wouldn't cushion the blow. His father was dead, his mother in a critical condition, and his daughters missing.

She would have to ask him awkward questions, intrusive at times. How does anyone deal with that?

CHAPTER NINE

Marsha and her family had taken their vehicles to Prophet and Son family-owned garage for as long as she could remember. The business had a good reputation and had doubled in size since Dan had taken over when John retired almost two years ago.

'What's going on, Marsha?' Dan ran a hand through his hair. 'Lucy said she can't get near to the house and—'

'Come with me, Dan, and I'll take you to her.'

'But—'

She beckoned him forwards, saying nothing to him.

It was as if his feet were stuck to the ground. Eventually, his brain kicked into gear, and he walked with her, down to the barn. When they were far enough away that they had a bit of privacy, she broke the news to him.

'No.' Dan dropped to one knee, holding his head in his hands.

'I'm so sorry for your loss.'

'But I only saw him yesterday. How did it happen?'

'Let's get you to Lucy, and I'll explain everything to you then.'

She helped him to his feet and they went to the barn. Inside, he ran straight into Lucy's arms.

Marsha stood to one side with Jess, giving the couple space as they cried together. It cut her to the core, but she never showed it was bothering her.

Her phone rang, and she went outside to take the call. It was from her DCI, Ryan Dixon. She updated him on all the details, sensing he would be as shocked as she was. As well as knowing John Prophet, too, Ryan had twin six-year-old granddaughters.

'Any sign of the girls yet?' he asked.

'No, sir. There are officers arriving as we speak, but the property is set in ten acres. Luckily, it isn't a working farm, so there are no animals roaming freely. Even so, it could be some time before we spot them, that's if they're still here.'

'You think they've been taken?'

'There's nothing suggesting that at the moment. Until we've searched the land, we won't know for sure. At least the weather is dry, but those girls will need water soon in this heat.'

'I'll send every available officer to you – I'll be with you soon, too. In the meantime, take the girls' parents away from the crime scene. Send me their address, and I'll get the ball rolling for a family liaison officer to meet you there. See what you can get from the Prophets beforehand, as well. I'll be there in twenty.'

Marsha disconnected the call and took a moment. More officers were arriving, the search team was being co-ordinated. Every inch of the place would be looked at, no stone unturned.

She glanced up at the gates. At least now the cordon had been moved further down the lane there were no cameras on them, but she wouldn't put it past someone to be sneaking around the perimeter of the property to get in another way.

Marsha rejoined them inside the barn. Jess was sitting across from Dan and Lucy, on bales of hay that had been fetched by one of them.

Marsha sat next to Jess. 'Dan, Lucy. Once again, I'm so sorry for your loss. I want you to know that we will do our best to draw this to a conclusion for you as quickly as possible. In order to do that, I need to ask a few direct questions. Okay?'

'Yes. Of course.' Dan wiped at his cheeks and sniffed.

'Firstly, let's get the worst of them out of the way. Is there anything you can tell me about why someone would do this to your parents?'

'No, I don't have a clue. I really don't.'

'When was the last time you saw them?'

'Yesterday. We had lunch together, at The Station in Rushton Spencer.'

Lucy gave a sob, and he squeezed her hand, shushing her gently.

'And there was nothing unusual? No strange moods between them, or people in the background you noticed? Your parents chatting to anyone you didn't know?' Marsha went on.

'No, nothing.'

Marsha made a note to speak to the proprietor. There might be something someone there could have noticed. Maybe a vehicle following Mr and Mrs Prophet senior.

Marsha had seen John and Sylvia Prophet recently at a community event. She'd presented John with an award for best local business. It was an award where the public could nominate a community member, and then judges would make the final decisions. To Marsha, it had shown how well-liked John was as he'd won for a second time.

'When I spoke to your parents last month, John told me

he was enjoying his retirement, although your mum had him decorating the living room, which he wasn't too keen on.'

Marsha was making small talk to put them at ease. Herself, too. It was hard for her to imagine what had happened.

'Is there anything else you'd like to tell us?'

'Nothing, really.' Dan huffed. 'You know Dad, a pillar of the community.'

It was said with some pride but underlying malice, Marsha thought, putting her senses on alert. John had always seemed a gentleman to her and, from what she'd seen of the father and son together over the years, she'd spotted nothing out of the ordinary. Maybe they put on a front while they were at work.

She went through a few more routine questions, and then the barn door opened. Ryan popped his head around it. She got to her feet.

'Would you excuse me? I'll leave you with Jess to get any further details, and then we'll take you home.'

'Wait. We're not leaving,' Dan cried as Lucy shook her head vehemently.

'This is a crime scene, and I think it's best that you're somewhere else.'

'Not until the girls come back. They'll be hiding somewhere, and we want to be here when they're found.'

'We're not leaving,' Lucy insisted.

Marsha sighed inwardly. Of course she'd known this would happen, but equally, it was hard to enforce it. She had to be firm.

'As soon as we have news, you'll be my first port of call. But for now, we need to take you home. It will be too distressing for you to stay here. There's far too much going on.'

'What if they're found?'

'Then we'll bring them straight to you, I promise.'

Lucy sat shaking her head, Dan saying nothing. Marsha could tell he was wavering. Eventually, he nodded.

Relief flooded through Marsha. She didn't want to upset them but would have done if she'd felt the need.

She had a duty of care to every member of the Prophet family, alive or dead.

CHAPTER TEN

Marsha left the barn, making a mental note to send her own daughters a message once she had a second. Even though they were sixteen and eighteen, they would always be her little girls and, it was at times like these that she needed to know they were safe.

The DCI was dressed in a forensic suit when she reached him. At six foot two, he was heavily built with short greying hair, distinguished, and always seemed to be calm in these kinds of situations.

Marsha had worked with him on and off for ten years, and there wasn't much about each other they didn't know. If they hadn't found the girls by the end of the day, it would probably hit him when he went home that evening.

It would hit them all.

'How are they?' Ryan asked her, pulling on latex gloves. 'Tell you anything interesting?'

'Nothing, really. I can't imagine what they're going through. I'd like to accompany them when we do the formal identification for John, if you don't mind?'

'Of course.' Ryan shook his head in disbelief. 'What a

shock. I was only talking to him last weekend. I booked my car in for a service, and he'd popped in. I was surprised to see him. He said he couldn't rely on anyone to run the place when he wasn't there. I got the impression he wasn't joking either. But I guess it's hard to let go, having run a business for so long.'

'Yes, lots of people will miss him. He was a larger-than-life character.'

Ryan glanced around. 'Those two little girls had a huge area to run and hide in, if that's what they'd been able to do.'

In the distance, Marsha could see people from the Crime Scene Investigation Team going about their duties. Tom Sidworth was the forensic photographer, and Stacey Rigby a forensic officer. It was a shame Jess wouldn't get to chat with them today. But it meant getting covered up again and, like Ryan said, they really needed to get Dan and Lucy Prophet away from the scene.

She went back to the barn and ushered Jess to the door.

'You okay?'

'Yes, boss.'

'Not the welcome I had in mind for you on your first day.' Marsha gave a faint smile. 'I had light duties planned. Lunch to get to know the team, a drive around the patch to familiarise yourself with some of the hot spots.'

'Nothing like being thrown in the deep end,' Jess replied. 'Any news on the girls?'

'Nothing.' Marsha glanced at Dan and Lucy, still huddled together. 'We'll have to get them past the press, who no doubt will enjoy taking photos of them as we fly by.' She raised her eyebrows. 'All hail my tinted windows.'

'What do you think has happened, boss?'

'If I didn't know both men quite so well, I wouldn't rule out a family squabble getting out of hand. But I can't think of anything off the top of my head. We'll do some digging when we get back to the station. Unless you picked up on anything else?'

'No, nothing. It seems so random at the moment.' Jess shook her head. 'I hope they find the girls soon.'

They took a moment to survey the fields. The farm sloping down from the main road gave them ample views of the search team walking in a line. Nathan and Connor were in their midst, too.

'Right, better get a wriggle on. The quicker those girls are found, the better for all concerned.' Marsha paused. 'I'll get Nathan and Connor to visit the neighbouring properties, along with some uniformed officers. Someone might have spotted something unusual, and if so, at least that might give us a time of death while we wait for the post-mortem to be done. Oh, talk of the devil.' Marsha nodded towards the car that was coming towards them. 'Here's Ruby now. She's the pathologist.'

They watched her park and retrieve her gear from the back of her car.

Ruby waved when she spotted Marsha.

In her late fifties, she had grey hair, with a hint of violet washed through it, tied back in a long plait. She wore the bare minimum of make-up, although her lips were the colour of a good red wine, to go with her name, she always said, and denim dungarees and a T-shirt, pink Crocs on her feet.

'Sorry, I'm a tad late,' she said. 'I was at my daughter's, playing with my grandson in the sandpit, so I didn't have time to go home and change.' She blew her fringe away from her forehead. 'Ridiculously hot today, isn't it? Who's this?'

Marsha smiled at her straightforward nature. 'DC Jess Baxter, meet the legend that is Ruby Wainwright.'

'Oh, behave.' Ruby laughed and held out her hand. 'I'm too old to be memorable anymore.'

Marsha tutted. 'Don't believe a word of it, Jess.' She

pointed at Ruby. 'This woman has saved my skin many a time over the years. She is a genius, I tell you.'

'Flattery will get you everywhere,' Ruby remarked, then made for the house. 'Now, show me the body. Is it a gruesome one?'

'Before you march off, it's someone you'll probably know,' Marsha warned.

Ruby stopped in her tracks and turned back.

'John Prophet.'

'From the garage?' Ruby sighed, her shoulders drooping. 'That's a shame. I wonder if it will close. I'd hate to take my car anywhere else.'

'Get your priorities right, why don't you.' Marsha smirked.

'Always.' Ruby waved and walked away again.

'She seems... direct,' Jess stated.

Marsha nodded her agreement. She liked the woman, and in the roles they did, a little humour was always necessary.

'She is, you'll get used to her.'

'Are you coming with me?' Ruby shouted to Marsha as she got to the front door of the property.

'I need to take the victim's son and daughter-in-law home.'

'Shame, I'd quite like to see you looking like a snowman with a bright-red face after sweating in the suit.'

'Ha, saved from mortification. I've seen as much as I can bear, to be honest. I don't know how you do your job at the best of times, but not at all when it's someone you know.'

Ruby smiled. 'All in the mindset, my love. All in the mindset.'

'Boss?'

Marsha turned to see Nathan jogging over. 'Anything?' she asked.

'Nothing yet, but the land is vast. We've checked all the outbuildings, though, and possible places the girls could hide.'

'Where are they?' Marsha groaned. 'It's getting hotter by

the minute. Let's hope someone has found them and taken them in. Can you and Connor talk to the neighbours either side and in the cottages across the way? Take some uniformed officers with you, to search their outbuildings, with their permission.'

'On it, boss.' He reached in his car for a bottle of water, almost drinking it in one go. 'I needed that.'

Now that everyone had been updated, Marsha knew it was time to get going. She clapped.

'Let's crack on, people. We can deal with the murder and assault as and when things come in. For now, we need to find Tamara and Maisie and bring them home.'

CHAPTER ELEVEN

Nathan opened the gate that would lead him to Ivy Cottage. It was another property that was mostly invisible from the road, down a steep bank.

He walked along the driveway with admiration, grass either side for as far as his eyes could see, thinking how he'd love to own a property like this one day. It was bound to have a few acres attached at the back, too.

The house was a detached stone cottage. It seemed newly renovated with square cream windows, and a large oak front door. He glanced around for any dogs that might be loose but, thankfully, he couldn't see any.

There was an old tractor next to a barn on the right, its doors closed, and a huge stack of logs piled up along one side. Even without the Prophet girls missing, the pull to go and have a rummage inside it was real.

At the door, Nathan rang the bell and then checked his phone while he waited for it to be answered. He had barely scrolled through an email when a woman in her early thirties opened the door. She was slim, black hair tied away from her face, wearing cut-off jeans and a white V-necked T-shirt.

Her smile was welcoming, and he returned it.

'Morning.' Nathan held up his warrant card. 'DS Clark. Sorry to disturb you, but we're investigating an incident at the neighbouring property, Dairy Croft Farm.'

'Oh, right, how can I help? Please, come in.'

He stepped inside a light and airy space, a row of coats and wellies along one wall, with a long wooden bench shaped like a church pew in between them, and a bank of doors on the other. Nathan followed the woman through to the kitchen.

'Would you like coffee? And a piece of cake? I've not long baked it – chocolate, with vanilla cream icing?'

He knew he shouldn't but if he was quick he could fit it in. And who could resist cake, even this early in the morning?

'Yes, that would be lovely. Black for me, one sugar, please.'

He walked a couple of steps over to the edge of the room, the sun streaming in making him squint.

'Lovely property you have,' he added, 'and what a view.' His gaze travelled over the patio area that led out to a lawn as big as a field. In the distance, the land sloped up again, covered in bushes and trees.

'Thanks.' The woman smiled at him as she sliced two pieces of cake. 'We've been here for about ten years, and the place is only just finished. I'm an interior designer and I feel like I want to start again in some of the rooms now. You mentioned an incident next door? I haven't been out yet, nor had the radio on. Is it something I should be concerned about?'

'I'm sorry to inform you that one of your neighbours was found dead this morning, and another injured.'

The woman's hand shot up to her mouth, and she staggered slightly.

'Are you okay, Mrs...?' Nathan enquired. 'Come and sit down for a moment.'

'Samantha.' She took his hand. 'Samantha Morgan.'

They sat at the table while the woman regained her composure enough to ask which person had died.

'I'm afraid we can't give out names yet until the formal identification has taken place, but the male is deceased, and the female was found injured. She's been taken to hospital.' He paused, not sure how to tell her the next part. 'Their granddaughters were staying over with them, and they weren't at the house when we arrived.'

'They've been taken?' Samantha was horrified.

'We're not certain yet. They may have run to hide, and we have officers searching for them. Do you have any outbuildings that they might be in?'

'We have the barn and the garage, that's it. I doubt any little girls would have got inside either of them. They're both locked due to the number of thefts around the area, and there are no windows open either. You're more than welcome to look, though.'

'Thank you.'

Samantha got up as the kettle boiled. Once drinks were made, she brought them over with the cake.

'I can't stomach this now, but you're welcome to a slice.'

Nathan refused, cursing inwardly. It felt rude to enjoy it now after all.

Samantha paused then. 'Missing, did you say? That's terrible news. We're trying to start a family, but I do wonder if it's a good idea to bring children into a world so dark.'

'I have a four-year-old girl, Daisy, and I worry about her every day. Still, I have to think that not everyone is out to cause people harm. There are a lot of nice folk around, too.'

Samantha smiled faintly.

'There will be a police presence over the next few days as we go about our investigation. It may be a little disruptive on a narrow road like this one.'

'Hardly inconvenient after what's happened. I must call my husband to let him know. He's in Italy at the moment. He flew out yesterday.'

'What does he do?'

'He has his own marketing firm.'

Nathan thought that made sense. Two creatives together. No wonder they could afford a place like this.

'Can you think back over the past few days to anything unusual you've seen? It might be something and nothing, big or small, but it could help?'

Samantha sipped at her coffee while she gave it some thought.

'There's a field between us and the Prophets, so I can't see much of their property. But there was a small white van parked across our drive on Friday. It was there for about an hour. I only know because I'd been baking and noticed it before I started. It was still there when I'd finished.'

'What type of van, would you know?'

'Not really, but it was small, the kind with two seats. It looked more like an estate car. It wasn't kept well, seemed to be falling apart. I walked up to ask if the driver needed help, but as I approached, it moved away.'

'Did you see who was driving, or how many people were in the vehicle?'

'Sorry, no. I wasn't close enough, and I didn't think to get a number plate. But come to think of it now, you can see right across Dairy Croft Farm from there. It gives a wide view of the drive and the house.'

Nathan was ready to leave. 'I'll get the search team to come immediately. Thank you so much for your help.'

'Not a problem. I do hope they find those girls soon.'

As soon as he got outside, Nathan rang Emma and asked her to check out CCTV in the area, from around the time of the murder. He had a feeling the white van might be a significant find.

CHAPTER TWELVE

Dan and Lucy Prophet lived in Longsdon, a small village four miles outside Leek, in a detached house situated within ample grounds.

Marsha took it all in as she drove down another long drive, towards a prominent property. Double-fronted with a porch at its middle, it had cream rendered walls and windows with sage-coloured frames. They parked up to the side.

Inside, they stepped into a large hall and, from there, were shown into a kitchen fitted with sleek, cream handleless units and marbled tops. The view showed fields for as far the eye could see. Marsha wanted to say something about it all but felt it wasn't appropriate. No one knew yet whether Tamara and Maisie had been kidnapped, and if so, it could be because they lived in a property like this.

'Have you been here long?' she asked instead.

'Eight years,' Dan said.

'I was seven months pregnant with Tam when we moved in.'

Tears welled up in Lucy's eyes, and Marsha knew that now was not the time to put any more questions to them. Instead, she asked if she could look around the house and the girls' bedrooms.

'Of course,' Dan replied. 'I'm not sure what you'll find, but if it will help...'

'Thanks.' Marsha nodded. 'Jess, why don't you stay here? I'll be as quick as I can.'

It was like stepping into an episode of *Escape to the Country*. But for all that, as Marsha wandered from room to room, it felt more like a home than a house, even though there wasn't a thing out of place.

She wondered if that was because of Dan or Lucy. Was one of them in control of the other or had demons from years gone by? Excessively tidy people often had something in their lives they felt the need to dominate.

Upstairs, Tamara's and Maisie's names were stencilled on doors opposite each other on a wide landing, but Marsha couldn't help having a peep into the other rooms first.

What appeared to be the master bedroom was huge, with a floor-to-ceiling window, and there was that view again.

It seemed to be occupied by them both if the books either side of the bed were anything to go by. Even so, she checked the two spare rooms and could see no sign that the couple were sleeping separately. Having said that, it wasn't always a sign of an unhappy marriage when couples had their own rooms.

In Maisie's bedroom, Marsha's heart went in her mouth as she looked around a pink palace similar to the decor that Cassie had had in her room until she'd found boy bands. Full of sparkle, with a disco ball light and unicorn bedding. Marsha imagined a four-year-old spending a lot of time in there.

There was nothing out of place, and she didn't really have a reason to search the rooms for now, so she left it and went into Tamara's. Her room was decked out in silvers, lilacs, and a few shades of purple, a little more grown up than her sister's, but still with a young-girl vibe. A teddy bear on the bed caught her attention as it was similar to the one in Maisie's room.

Marsha felt a twang of longing for her daughters to be young again. For life not to be moving so quickly. The need to bring the Prophet girls home to these comfortable surroundings, where, from what she could see, they were loved and cherished, was overwhelming.

A noise alerted her to someone coming up the stairs, and she turned to see Jess standing in the doorway.

'The FLO is here, boss,' Jess said quietly.

Marsha went down to greet the family liaison officer, who was waiting in the hall. She smiled as she recognised her. Having worked with her twice before, she'd found both experiences to be good.

PC Rachel Joy was twenty-six, with long blonde hair she always tied up out of the way. Marsha said hello, and they went into the kitchen. Dan and Lucy were sitting at the breakfast bar.

Marsha introduced Rachel to them and explained what would happen now.

'Rachel will be your first port of call if you want anything, or if you think of something that we need to know,' Marsha added. 'She'll also be my contact if I have to tell you something. But I'm always available to call direct.' She got out a card and popped it on the surface in front of them.

'I need to ask you some difficult questions now. They may feel intrusive, but they are necessary.' She held up a hand at their shocked expressions. 'It's routine, that's all. Can I ask you both where you were this morning from eight to nine a.m.?'

'I was in Buxton first thing,' Dan said. 'I had an order to pick up for an urgent job and left the house at about seven. I was driving back when Lucy rang me to say she couldn't get to my parents' home.' He paused. 'I stopped for diesel on my way back.'

'Do you have the receipt?'

'Yes, it's in my wallet.' He got it out and gave it to her.

Marsha could see the time and date. They would check CCTV at the garage as well, but it was looking likely he was in the clear.

'And you, Lucy?'

'I was here until nine, and then I went to pick up the girls.'

'Did you stop off anywhere on the way?'

'No.' Her eyes went down momentarily, her skin reddening slightly.

Marsha noted it.

Once she felt able to leave, it was nearly one-thirty. She and Jess needed to get back to the station.

'Wow,' Jess exclaimed. 'Business must certainly be booming for the family.'

'Indeed. I haven't heard any rumours about them being involved in anything sinister, but Emma will be delving into their financial backgrounds.'

'Nice gaff, inside and out, though.' Jess buckled her seatbelt.

'Gorgeous. I have a fair-sized house but I'm not sure I'd want one that big. Imagine all the cleaning.'

'Not to mention the heating bills.'

They grinned at each other, both aware they were making mountains out of molehills. To have the sort of money that the Prophet family had was a dream that most people aspired to, despite the problems the size of the house might bring. Whether a lot of people were happy when they had it was another thing entirely. They saw the downsides only too often in their profession, too.

'What do you make of the couple?' Marsha asked.

Jess's lips went down either side of her mouth. 'They seem okay to me. No airs and graces, considering how wealthy they are.'

'A good marriage?'

'I'm afraid I don't have any experience on that front, but from what I can see, I think so. What about you?'

'I'm not sure. I saw Lucy blush after we asked her whereabouts, and the house seemed a bit neat, but then, you should see my house. It's a tip most days!'

'It's a happy home, though?'

Marsha nodded. For the most part, it was.

CHAPTER THIRTEEN

The street was quiet. Most people would be at work, but he walked swiftly. He pictured how the families behind the doors of the homes he passed lived. Happy, caring parents with wonderful loving children. A dog and a cat. Trips away in the sun during the summer holidays. Football games and ballet lessons. Things he'd never had, nor ever would.

He had no remorse for what he'd done. No emotion either. He'd taken a life, an eye for an eye. The woman had been a mistake, and the girls? An even bigger one. But he couldn't have left them at the house. They would have identified him too easily. He needed more time.

The newsagent's on the corner, that he remembered as a boy, was now a mini mart. Aisles too close together, rammed with everything for convenience, even though there was competition from a large supermarket a few streets away.

A weedy man with a receding hairline stood behind the counter, scrolling through his phone, not taking a blind bit of notice of the shop. A woman with a child in a pushchair was hogging one aisle.

He squeezed past to make a point, glaring at her, but she

didn't move an inch out of his way. She didn't spot him, too busy on her phone, too. Her voice was shrill. It was a good thing the call wasn't confidential as everyone for miles around would hear what her best friend, Denise, had been up to the night before.

People were so weird nowadays, he mused, bragging about everything all over social media, telling anyone who'd listen how well they were doing. Not that he'd ever been able to do that. He hadn't had a good job for years. Everything was temporary, or backbreaking work for a pittance.

He picked up sandwiches, crisps and chocolate, and bottles of water. A small loaf for himself, more butter and coffee, a packet of biscuits, and two tins of baked beans. That would tide him over. He wasn't going to be there long. The doctors had given his father a week at most to live, and once the funeral had taken place, he would be on his way again.

If it wasn't for his mum dying, he wasn't sure he'd have come back at all. He wasn't close to his parents and siblings; hadn't even known his mum had been ill until it was too late. And now his dad was in a hospice receiving palliative care. Neither he, nor his mum, had reached their sixtieth birthdays.

His dad had rung him when he'd been taken into hospital. A week later, he'd been transferred to a hospice for specialist care. It had been the last straw.

The woman with the buggy was still talking on the phone when he got to the till, her kid screeching his unhappiness now.

He paid for his shopping, no one taking any notice of what was in his basket. Without a backwards glance, he was on his way home again.

He was calm as he walked back. On the corner of his street, he caught the conversation of two women who had stopped to chat. He recognised them both as living close to him.

'It's all over the news, Michelle,' one said. 'I can't believe it. I hope the little girls are okay.'

'Me, too, love,' the other replied. 'It's shocking. Makes me scared to go out.'

He smiled, to put them at ease. Then he chuckled to himself once he continued on his way.

They hadn't got a clue. It was nice to be one step ahead for a change.

He let himself into the house. It was quiet, which was good. The girls would probably realise soon that he wasn't taking them to the police, or to their parents. And then he'd have to hope they'd behave themselves.

CHAPTER FOURTEEN

Nathan and Connor had been back at the station for half an hour and were having a late lunch at their desks. Before Marsha did anything, she sent a message to Suzanne saying she hoped she was having a good day, and then one to Cassie asking how her exam had gone. Cassie was sitting her final GCSEs that week. She'd had several exams already, with only a few to go.

At last, she could tuck into the sandwich she'd grabbed when she'd filled up with diesel on the way back. Jess had opted for a box of fruit and a yoghurt.

Emma had made them all drinks and was dishing them out. The mood in the office was sombre, nothing like it had been earlier in the day.

A message beeped in on Marsha's phone. It was from Cassie.

Maths was boring, but at least it's done! Only three more exams to go! x

Marsha grinned. She'd never been good at maths herself and could clearly remember the elation of walking out of the hall after the exam and punching the air, glad that it was over.

'Something good, boss?' Emma asked.

'Just a message from Cassie, saying how relieved she is that her exams are nearly finished. It was maths today.'

'I hated that. All those algebra things that I've never used since the day I left school.'

'I still can't understand the point of half of it,' Connor joined in. 'We'd be better teaching our kids how to budget during a cost-of-living crisis, and how to get through a rough patch when your mortgage or rent rockets sky-high. That would be much more useful.'

'All I can say is, I'm glad I'm not starting out now,' Nathan added.

Once Marsha was finished, she wiped her hands and went to stand in front of the digital screen. While they'd been out, Emma had added lots of things to it. Photos of the deceased and his wife, and Tamara and Maisie Prophet, were prominent in a line at the top.

There were a few images of Dairy Croft Farm, and John's body before it had been moved, plus several scenes from the hallway. The timeline on the whiteboard had been marked with the first call to emergency services, in readiness for what was to come.

'Right, let's crack on, shall we? The DCI is still on scene and likely to remain there until about four p.m. Sadly, the girls haven't been found yet, even though the farm buildings and the land have been thoroughly searched.

'Tamara, the eldest girl, has a mobile phone. We've tried calling it several times with no answer. We'll keep trying, but with no sightings, we'll be asking anyone in the vicinity to check all their outbuildings. Ryan is hosting a press conference at six-thirty. Hopefully, the girls are hunkered down, too scared to come out of hiding.'

'How were the Prophets?' Emma asked, finishing the last of her drink.

'It was tough to be in the home with them, as beautiful as it is. They seem numb, confused as to why this has happened to them. The family liaison officer assigned is PC Rachel Joy, from Stoke. She was there when we left. Connor, what have you got for us?'

'I spoke to several neighbours, in a row of cottages further up the lane, but no one reported seeing anything out of the ordinary. They all just expressed their condolences and shock. But the owner of Berry Lane Farm said he'd hired an odd-job man last week. He'd arrived on foot and was asking for work. He paid him twenty pounds to shift a pile of scrap metal.'

'Description?'

'White, around six foot with short blond hair. About forty.'

'So he was there for that day only?'

'A couple of hours at the most.'

'And does that give a view of Dairy Croft Farm?'

'It does, but not as good as from the top of the lane.'

'Okay, thanks. Nathan?'

He relayed the details about his visit to Ivy Cottage.

'So someone could have been staking out the farm,' Marsha mused. 'Emma, it's going to be a long trawl, but we need to get CCTV from the main road to see if we can trace the vehicle back.'

'Already on it, boss,' Emma replied. 'Nathan called me when the neighbour reported seeing the white van.'

'Great work, you two. Thanks.' Marsha glanced around. 'Any more for any more?'

When nothing was forthcoming, she rounded things off. 'I need actions creating for things we'll be following up on. For now, we'll concentrate on the missing girls. Let's look into both couples' backgrounds in more detail. See if there's anything we don't know about. Also, we need to talk to the workforce at the garage. They've been sent home today, so that might be better to do first thing when the business is open again.'

She checked her watch.

'As I mentioned earlier, the DCI is putting out a quick TV bulletin this evening, and then a further update at nine a.m. tomorrow. Post-mortem results are also due in the morning, and I'm taking Dan and Lucy to ID the body. I think they have enough to worry about this evening with Sylvia in hospital and their little girls missing.'

'Shall I visit the staff at the garage first thing?' Jess offered.

'I was going to do that with Connor,' Nathan stated.

Marsha's eyes turned sharply at his tone. It was unusual for him to snap like that. She nodded at Jess.

'You can go with Nathan, Jess. In the hope that the girls are found by the morning, we can then concentrate on finding John Prophet's killer. Someone will need to speak to Mrs Prophet, too, when she's awake. They're monitoring her in case she needs to be put into an induced coma, but she's stable and sedated for now.'

'Do we know what caused her injury yet?' Connor asked.

'It still seems like she was pushed hard, fell, and hit her head on the wall. Most likely she was trying to ward off the attacker, stop him from hurting her husband, and perhaps getting to the girls.'

They sat in silence for a few seconds, each with their own thoughts. It was hard to get their heads around. As a team, they weren't usually on scene before the forensic staff arrived. Seeing it all first-hand was a bit too close for comfort, to say the least.

'I think we have a few questions here.' Marsha used her fingers to count them out. 'One, did someone or some persons, go to Dairy Croft Farm to attack or murder John Prophet? Two, did they go to attack or murder both John *and*

Sylvia? Three, did an argument between family members get out of hand, or other people, come to think of it? And four, was taking the girls the priority, and their grandparents tried to stop their abduction?'

Marsha shuddered at the thought. She looked around at the sullen faces once her words had sunk in. She prayed Tamara and Maisie hadn't been kidnapped.

Another message came in on her phone, and she quickly reached for it. With a sigh of relief, she saw it was from Suzanne.

Day going well, ta. Not like yours! I saw the news. Hope those girls are found soon. See you later. x

'We're going to find out who attacked the Prophet family,' she said to rally the team. 'And we're going to bring those girls home.'

CHAPTER FIFTEEN

Lucy Prophet sat down on Maisie's bed and picked up the soft toy that was on the pillow. Maisie had recently grown out of her furry friends, finding dolls and Lego far more interesting, but Lucy was glad she hadn't wanted to say goodbye to Barney. He was a lemon teddy bear that they'd bought Maisie when she was born. He'd been washed several times to stop him looking grimy and wore a pink T-shirt with Maisie's name, and date of birth, embroidered on it. Tamara had one, too.

She ran a hand over its fur before bringing it to her chest, squeezing it tightly. She wasn't sure she'd stopped crying since that morning, yet she and Dan couldn't even begin to grieve for his dad until they knew what had happened to the girls.

Had they run away and were hiding, or had someone taken them? Her life would be unbearable without Tamara and Maisie. She stared out of the window, over the garden and into the fields beyond. Eight years ago, they had been so proud to move into this house. It had everything they wanted. Before that had come the heartache of trying to start a family.

It had taken three rounds of IVF for her to conceive Tamara. She'd been seven months pregnant when they'd moved in and had been banned from doing anything. A removal firm had packed everything at their last home and unpacked it in the new one. It had felt intrusive, but she hadn't wanted to tempt fate, not after getting that far at last.

Tamara arrived two weeks early and was the icing on the cake for her and Dan. They were besotted. They'd tried again naturally afterwards, but it had taken two further rounds of IVF before Maisie came along. They were lucky. Dan's parents paid for most of it by giving him generous bonuses.

Many barren years had meant they were older parents, though. They didn't have much in common with their friends whose children were now teenagers, nor the younger mums who were in their late twenties. It had left Lucy in a bit of limbo. But, gradually, she had made one or two acquaintances.

It couldn't all be over. She wouldn't allow those thoughts to slip into her head.

The door opened, and Dan came into the room. Without a word, he sat next to her.

'Any news?' she asked.

It was a silly thing to say. Lucy knew he would have told her if so.

'Nothing yet.' He put an arm around her shoulders. 'They've just put out an appeal. Did you hear it on the radio?'

'Yes. Usually, I listen to those bulletins without a care in the world. Well, not literally. I'm always sympathetic and worried for the children. But as it's happening to someone else, it feels as if it will never affect us. I can't believe they were talking about Tamara and Maisie. Is she still here?'

Lucy was referring to the family liaison officer. Although Rachel seemed nice, while she kept them informed of what was going on, Lucy didn't like someone she didn't know in her home.

'Yes,' Dan said. 'She's offered to stay the night if we need her to.'

'Do they do that?'

'Sometimes. She wants to be close in case there's any progress.'

'I don't want her here, Dan.'

'If it helps, she'll have to stay. I know it's uncomfortable, but the police are out there now, trying to find our girls. If – when they do, they'll tell her first. If she wasn't here, we might not get that call straight away.'

Lucy doubted anyone would keep them hanging, but she knew what he was getting at. Rachel was a necessity for now.

'I suppose she could sleep in the guest room,' she relented.

'I wish I could go to the farm.' Dan paused. 'If there's no news by the morning, I'm going up there regardless.'

'They won't let you near.'

'I'll keep away from the house. They can't stop me searching the land. But I have to do something.'

Lucy pulled a tissue from her pocket and wiped her nose. 'It's going to be strange tonight if... if... where are they, Dan?' She broke down in tears. 'Where are our girls?'

'We'll find them,' Dan soothed, his voice choked with emotion. 'We'll find them.'

Dan left Lucy asleep on Maisie's bed and went into their bedroom. The heat was stifling, so he took a quick shower. Under the water, he let his tears flow. His father was dead, his mum was in hospital, and his girls were missing. Who would do such a thing to their family, and more to the point, why?

For as long as he lived, he would never forget the call that came from Lucy. She'd been frantic, and he hadn't been able to absorb what she was saying. Something about the police being at the farm and that she couldn't get in to see what was going on.

Although he'd been halfway home from Buxton, he'd left everything he'd collected in his van rather than dropping the order off at the garage, putting his foot down to get to his parents' home. And then he'd heard everything from the police.

Rachel said she would take them to see his mum as soon as it was okay to do so. The latest update was that her head was swollen where she'd taken the bang to it, and she had bruising on her back and arm, too, where she'd fallen. She was sedated for now, but, after losing his father, Dan needed to see that she was still alive.

She was going to be distraught when she woke up. If she had no permanent damage to her brain, that was. Until she regained consciousness, no one could be certain.

Ever since he'd heard the news, he'd been trying to think who could have done this to his family. There might be a number of people from years gone by who'd been aggrieved by his dad.

For the first few years John was in business in the eighties, things hadn't been run that well. He'd started off with lots of old cars and vans, most of which weren't even roadworthy the minute they left the garage. He'd been known for giving a good rate for a dodgy MOT certificate.

Yet, over the decades, Prophet and Son had become a business people could trust. The motors they sold were high-class now, their mechanics and bodywork second to none. Dan prided himself in giving good service. Their staff throughout the years had been the same.

He'd started working there straight from school, and two of the mechanics from back then were still with them now. That said a lot in this day and age, although things weren't quite all they seemed in the background. His father was known as a hard man to work for.

So the question he was asking himself, over and over, was, had someone set out to harm his dad because of something that had happened in the past?

Or was someone getting back at *him*?

CHAPTER SIXTEEN

Marsha was downstairs, outside the press conference room with Jess. They were waiting in the corridor to see Ryan before he addressed the camera for an appeal to the public.

The noise was deafening as people streamed in ready to hear the update. It would be shown live on TV. Marsha prayed it would do the trick in getting everyone's attention rather than only those who had heard about it in real time.

As John Prophet was known to many locally, Ryan had checked with the family to see if they would approve releasing his name before the formal identification had taken place. Usually, they wouldn't divulge names, but in the vein that it may help find their daughters, Dan and Lucy were in agreement.

It was six thirty, and everyone was feeling the pressure. Despite an intensive search, there had been no sightings of Tamara or Maisie. Every available officer was out on the farm and surrounding areas.

Marsha and her team might find themselves back there tomorrow, now that everything had been set up at the station, interviewing people to see what evidence they could gather after the news broke in full.

'How are you feeling?' Marsha asked Jess.

'I'm good, thanks,' Jess replied.

'You've certainly been thrown in at the deep end today.' Marsha gave her a discreet smile to show her sympathy.

'It's one way to meet a lot of officers and other people that will no doubt be a part of my working life. Although I doubt I'll remember everyone's name!'

'Well, that's our press officer, Scarlett Hilton, coming towards us with the DCI. She's good to have on side and is especially skilled at nipping things in the bud, or only getting stuff into the press that we want people knowing about. She always takes a positive slant wherever possible, too. I'll introduce you later as I think we're about to go in.'

They followed Ryan and Scarlett into the room. At the far end, two long tables had been pushed together lengthways. Pull-up banners with the Staffordshire Police logos and important phone numbers stood either side behind them, and a lectern had been moved to the far wall out of the way.

In front were rows of chairs, at the moment full of local journalists and national press, with cameras, and recorders on phones, at the ready.

Ryan drew out a chair and sat down. Although Marsha could see sweat patches under his arms, she put it down to the hot weather. Things like this never seemed to faze him.

As the briefing was going to be a quick update, Ryan was doing it alone. Marsha was thankful. She disliked being on camera. She imagined it very much like being a suspect who was interviewed, a rabbit-in-headlights feeling.

Like all the team, she'd received press training, but even so, no matter how confident she felt about a subject, she would always become tongue-tied. She never said anything she shouldn't, but often couldn't form a sentence without either waffling or not making any sense.

She pointed to the side of the room, and she and Jess shuffled along into a gap. While Ryan got settled, Marsha glanced around to observe the press. There were some she liked; some not so much. Over the years, she'd worked out who she could trust and who she couldn't.

Marsha waved when Max Harvey, lead crime reporter at *Leek News*, caught her eye. He smiled back, then settled in his seat, getting himself ready.

Before she'd joined the police, Marsha had always thought she'd do work experience at their local paper before heading to Manchester. She had actually seen herself working there if she'd decided to stay in Leek. It would have been good to get a feel of the local demographics early on.

Now, however, she knew every street, every family of troublemakers, the good spots, the bad places – just as well as Max would know his patch as a journalist.

'Good afternoon, ladies and gentlemen,' Ryan began, and the room dropped into silence.

'Early this morning, police were called out to a disturbance at Dairy Croft Farm, Meerbrook Road. Once at the scene, sadly I can confirm the death of local businessman, John Prophet, sixty-nine. His wife, Sylvia, was also injured and is critical but stable in the Royal Stoke Hospital. There has been no formal identification yet, but as there are other developments, the family have allowed us to give out their names.

'John and Sylvia Prophet were looking after their granddaughters overnight. These two girls are now missing. We are not certain if they have been taken by the person, or persons, who committed the attacks on the couple. The children may have run to hide when their grandparents were being assaulted, and they may be too scared to be found.'

Ryan held up the image that Marsha had retrieved from Lucy Prophet's phone earlier. 'Eight-year-old Tamara has mousey brown hair, and we think she may be wearing denim shorts, a yellow T-shirt, and white Converse trainers. Four-year-old Maisie, we believe, is wearing a pink summer dress with daisies, and white sandals. These clothes were packed by their mother for them to wear.

'We are asking any member of the public in the area to check inside sheds, garages, outbuildings, caravans, camper vans, anywhere that these two little girls may be hiding. A thorough search of the land on and around the farm is taking place, but as yet, there have been no sightings.

'We would also like to speak to anyone who was in the vicinity of Dairy Croft Farm over the past few days. Our top priority is to find Tamara and Maisie. A murder and attempted murder inquiry has also been set up. We will not be taking questions at this moment in time, but there will be a further update at nine a.m. tomorrow. Thank you.'

Members of the audience shouted loudly to get his attention, but Ryan moved swiftly out of the room.

Marsha quickly followed behind him with Jess. They headed for the stairwell, out of the eye of the media.

'Hello again, Jess. Sorry I couldn't welcome you properly earlier on.' Ryan offered his hand before they took the steps to the first floor. 'Good to have you on board.'

'Thank you, sir.'

'Is everything set up?' Ryan looked at Marsha for confirmation.

'Yes, sir. Hopefully we'll get some sightings to check out this evening. My team are ready to take calls.'

'Right, well, keep me informed of any developments.'

'Sir.'

Marsha and Jess went back to the office. Nathan, Connor, and Emma were all heads down at their computers.

'Anything?' Marsha asked.

'Not about the girls, boss,' Emma replied. 'But FFU have come back with financial records, and there's nothing untoward in any of the personal or business accounts of either couple.'

Marsha took a quick skim through the details, agreeing with Emma.

'Okay, folks. Let's go to the incident room and lend a hand answering some phone calls. Hopefully the public will be good to us and give us the information we need.' Marsha sighed. 'Seems like it might be a long night.'

CHAPTER SEVENTEEN

Tamara Prophet sat on the bed with her arms around her sister, trying her best not to cry. She wanted to be brave, but her teeth were chattering, and it wasn't even cold.

They had been locked in the room for hours now. It wasn't a very nice place to be. There was only a bed, with a scruffy blanket, which they were sitting on top of. Flowery wallpaper in the corner was curling down as if it was going to fall off, and there were patches of it missing where someone seemed to have ripped it. There was no lampshade, and a lot of dust in the air if they moved.

'I want to go home, Tam.' Maisie sobbed into her chest. 'Why can't we go home?'

'Don't cry,' Tamara comforted. 'The man said we'd be safe here.'

'But that was *ages* ago. I don't want to stay here.'

Tamara didn't know what to say. At eight, she was old enough to know that the man was lying. Her parents weren't coming for them. The police weren't coming either. He was a bad man. It must have been him who had hurt her gran and granddad.

They shouldn't have left with him. They should have stayed in the house, ran and hid until he'd gone. But she had been scared, and the man said they'd be safer with him.

He'd taken them to his house, she didn't know where. Then he'd told them to run upstairs and hide in the back bedroom. He'd said to be quiet and to stay away from the window.

He'd closed the curtains, too. And when he'd left the room, he'd locked the door. Why had he done that? They would be too scared to leave.

'Are you hungry? Or thirsty?' she asked Maisie, getting off the bed to look again in the bag that he'd brought in for them. Inside it was sandwiches and crisps, bars of chocolate, and bottles of water. There was so much of it.

Maisie shook her head. 'I just want to go home.'

'We have to be brave, Maisie. Mummy and Daddy will come to get us soon, but until then, we have to be quiet.'

She listened to her sister's snuffles, holding back her own tears. She was so scared.

It was half an hour later when he came upstairs. Tamara swallowed as he unlocked the door.

He was a small man, with large hands. His face had stubble like Dad's when he hadn't had a shave in the morning. He was wearing the same clothes as he had on that morning, a dirty blue T-shirt and jeans.

'I'm afraid you need to stay here tonight, so it's time for you to go to sleep,' he said. 'You can use the bathroom again if you're quick.'

They froze.

'Come on, now.' His voice was sharper this time.

Tamara knew she wouldn't be able to hold herself until the morning, and neither would Maisie. She was desperate for the loo. So, even though she was scared to leave the room, she took hold of Maisie's hand, and they scrambled off the bed and onto the landing.

The bathroom was dirtier than the room they'd been kept in, black stuff between the tiles, and a smell that made her wrinkle up her nose. It didn't look as if it had been cleaned for ages.

Tamara used the toilet and waited while Maisie did the same.

'I need to brush my teeth.' Maisie glanced round, grimacing. 'There's no toothbrushes.'

'We'll have to pretend.' Tamara squeezed a bit of toothpaste on her index finger and rubbed it around her teeth. 'Like this, see?'

Maisie nodded, copying her.

'Hurry up. I haven't got all day.'

The man's voice made them jump, and they rushed back into the bedroom.

He closed the door behind him, and the key in the lock turned. Tamara felt safer somehow.

Maisie began to cry again, so Tamara wrapped her arms around her.

'I don't want to stay here tonight, Tam. I want to sleep in my own bed.'

'You need to behave, Maisie, and then he might let us go home tomorrow.'

'But I don't like the dark.'

'Close your eyes, and you won't see it then.'

It was a silly thing that Mum said to them, and it soothed Maisie for now.

Tamara needed to be brave, too. She missed her mum and dad so much, but she had to take care of Maisie. She was her big sister, and that was the most important thing. She had a job to do.

. . .

In the living room, he flopped onto the settee. He wanted a drink to calm him down, but he couldn't have any. He needed to be sober that evening.

Taking the girls wasn't part of the plan – how the hell was he supposed to know they'd be there? But he'd had no choice. They'd seen him. They could identify him. If he was caught, he wouldn't be able to get to everyone.

He'd almost snapped when he'd heard the little girl crying, the older one shushing her. He should let them go now, really. They were innocents in all this.

Then again, he'd been the same at one time, before one simple thing had changed his life forever. And someone had to pay for that. Well, not someone. Some people.

He watched the news reel again. It was coming on every quarter of an hour, photos of the girls and their grandparents flashing up every few minutes. He wouldn't be put off by it, but he needed to watch it to see what was happening. It might allow him to stay one step ahead.

The girl was crying louder now. He'd be in for it if the neighbours heard her, so he switched the TV up as loud as he could before it was at a level where they'd be round to complain. The walls were so thin between them. He could hear them flushing the loo first thing every morning, sometimes during the night.

He wondered what they'd think if they found out what was happening right under their noses. He laughed inwardly. Stuart Parker was okay, but his wife was a right nosy cow. She'd be mortified she'd missed her moment of glory. If she found the girls, she'd be all over the cameras, showing off and no doubt making lies up about him. Stupid bitch.

He clasped his hands over his ears and left them there for a couple of minutes. After that, he went to stand in the hall. He couldn't hear the girl now. Perhaps she'd settled down for the night.

Because he'd have to leave soon.

He'd only be gone for a couple of hours, and he'd slip out the back way so they wouldn't even realise they were alone.

For a second, he thought this wasn't what he was all about. He really should let them go. His argument wasn't with them.

Then he shook his head.

Stuff it. Besides, he had work to do that evening.

CHAPTER EIGHTEEN

It was half past ten when Marsha opened her front door. Inside the hall, she yawned before throwing her keys into the bowl on the sideboard. Larry came sauntering in to greet her, tail wagging against the stairs.

'Hey, boy.' She bent to give him a fuss.

Her shoulders sagged as she stared at herself in the mirror. Apart from a few scraps of mascara underneath her eyes, her make-up had all but gone. Her hair was a mess where she'd run her hands through it, something she did when she was stressed.

She hadn't expected to come home without knowing Tamara and Maisie were safe. Marsha hoped they would have found the girls by now, huddled together in a barn or outbuilding, afraid to come out even if they'd heard their names being shouted. After all, why would they trust anyone who was trying to find them? She couldn't begin to imagine what they had seen.

But it meant that lots of people would have a restless night. She knew for certain that she would see their little faces whenever she closed her eyes, not to mention the body of John Prophet and his poor wife, Sylvia.

Before she'd left the station, she'd rung the hospital for an update. Sylvia was still stable but doing better now, and they were hoping they'd be able to talk to her in the morning, when the sedation had worn off. For now, she was their only witness. The one person who could tell them what had happened.

In the front room, Marsha found Cassie lounging on the settee. Larry had jumped up beside her, no doubt back to his original place.

'Everything good?' she asked.

'Yep.'

'Where's your sister?'

'Working. She got offered another shift. She won't be long, though.' Cassie sat up and pulled her legs into one side. 'Have you found them?'

Marsha shook her head. 'Afraid not.'

'I spotted you on the news. You looked knackered.'

'Always the one to dish out the compliments, aren't you, love?' Marsha snorted. 'I feel it, though, to be honest. It's tough when kids go missing.'

'I can't believe John Prophet is dead. Do you know why yet? Or who it might be?'

'You know I can't tell you anything.'

'Spoilsport.' Cassie poked out her tongue and then grinned. 'I was about to make some toast. Want some?'

'Please.' Marsha dropped into the armchair. 'Is your dad in?'

'Gone to bed.'

Marsha huffed. It was typical that he was in while she'd been working late.

She reached for the TV remote and switched to the news

channel. Their case was flashed all over the yellow ticker tape that ran across the bottom of the screen.

She hated that it was headline news, but it was important that everyone got to learn about Tamara and Maisie Prophet. Tears welled in her eyes at the thought of what their parents were going through.

Marsha recalled losing Cassie in the shopping centre once, remembering how it felt as if her heart had dropped down into her stomach when she couldn't see her. She'd been searching for the right size T-shirt for Suzanne, and when she'd glanced around, Cassie was nowhere to be seen.

She'd found her twenty minutes later. While Marsha had been shouting at the top of her voice and running around in circles, someone had spotted Cassie in Claire's Accessories, notified a security guard, and it had been announced over the tannoy.

Marsha had never run so fast in her life to get to the information desk, where Cassie had been taken to. She sensed all eyes on her when she'd got there, all of a fluster, to find Cassie sitting on a chair, swinging her legs as she played with a hair brush that she hadn't paid for.

Tears of relief came then, along with a few choice words to her daughter. Cassie must have wandered across there, tempted by their bright colours, while her back was turned. It was so easily done, but she could have been taken just as quickly, too.

Marsha had never forgotten that feeling, the fear that coursed through her. It had come back to her numerous times throughout her career, but nothing was ever as frightening as that moment.

On the TV, the news channel was replaying Ryan's briefing about their case. The camera then switched to Meerbrook Road, down from the farmhouse. Thankfully, the press and their vehicles were far away enough not to be too intrusive. The neighbours needed access to their homes, too, plus their privacy.

Cassie came back in the room and handed her a plate of toast and a mug of tea. Larry sat up to investigate.

'Ta, love.' Marsha groaned after taking the first bite. 'Heaven. I'm starving. How did the revision go this evening?'

'Okay. I'll be glad when it's all over.'

'And you'll have a whole summer to enjoy before college. Plus a week in Corfu.'

As a family, they went to the island every July. It was always too hot, and busy, as it had to be during the school holidays, but Marsha had still loved it. Until recently. Now she was dreading a week where she and Phil would have to pretend to be sociable while with their girls.

She'd wanted this holiday to be special, knowing that it was more than likely the last one they would have as a family. Suzanne was too old to go with her parents, and she'd most probably be going with friends or her boyfriend soon.

They might get a couple more years with Cassie, but even so, three out of four just wouldn't be the same. Her girls were close, despite their quarrels and tantrums every now and then, and they kept each other company

Marsha was worried that Cassie would be lonely without her sister. Still, that was next year's problem. This year's was whether she and Phil would get along okay.

She shared some of her toast with Larry and then took him out for a quick walk. Finally, unable to put off the obvious, she said goodnight to Cassie and went upstairs.

Phil was sitting up, watching TV. When she got into bed, he switched it off. The silence was deafening and awkward as hell.

'Is there something wrong?' she asked eventually. 'You don't usually turn the TV off when I come upstairs. You just grunt and carry on watching it.'

'We need to talk.'

'About what?'

'Us.'

Marsha couldn't help but snigger. She wasn't sure there was an *us* anymore, and she supposed she needed to listen. But now wasn't the right time. She couldn't cope with anything personal today.

'It's late, can it wait?'

Phil sighed. 'Shall I book an appointment to see you? How about this weekend?' Or perhaps next month?'

'You pick your moments, don't you? I'm in the middle of a murder inquiry with a woman assaulted and two missing kids and—'

'I don't care about your stupid job,' he snapped. 'I want to talk about you and me.'

'Well, I'm not in the mood.' Marsha slid down the bed and turned over, keeping her back to him. She squeezed her eyes shut, the tears she refused to let fall burning them. She wouldn't show him how hurt she was.

Because all she wanted to do was bury her head in the sand, and pretend that her marriage might not be over.

CHAPTER NINETEEN

On the drive home, Jess thought about her first day. She hadn't wanted it to be so hectic but, like she'd said to Marsha, crime never stopped just because she wanted to settle in somewhere first.

Even so, she wondered what her new team thought of her so far. She liked Marsha, which was a huge bonus, and had enjoyed going out with her. Emma was nice, too, and Connor.

Nathan had been a bit tetchy, and she wasn't sure why, but hopefully that would disappear in time. She hoped everyone liked her really, otherwise her job would be hard from the start.

Under the circumstances, everything had gone well. They hadn't found the missing girls, and it was early days, but she knew that things pieced together at the beginning of an investigation added up over the coming days, enabling them to create a larger picture of what had happened.

Apprehending suspects was something Jess loved to do, and this case in particular was playing on her heartstrings. One day she wanted to have children of her own.

She pulled in the driveway at her mum's house and parked

up, killing the engine and sitting for a moment. In contrast to what she'd been used to in Manchester, it was deadly quiet.

Here, she could hear an owl hooting in the distance, a ripple of a breeze through the trees, and nothing else.

Here, she felt safe.

There, she would be serenaded by emergency vehicle sirens at all times of the day and evening. She'd be mindful of where she parked on a night out and be wary of the drunks walking home from the many pubs and clubs afterwards.

'Is that you, love?' Pam shouted through when she finally went indoors.

Jess was tempted to ask her who else it would be but kept the words to herself. She was shattered and grumpy. No need to take it out on someone else.

'Yes, it's me,' she said.

Pam appeared in the doorway in her pyjamas, a steaming mug of tea in her hand. 'I heard the news, such a tragedy. Those poor little girls. Have you found them yet?'

'No, Mum. We're still looking.'

'Oh, that's terrible.' Pam clutched her chest. 'Do you know what happened to the man who died?'

'I can't talk about it.' Jess went through to the kitchen.

'I'm just showing concern.' Pam sounded aggrieved.

Jess wished it was only that. Her mum was a gossip. She'd be straight around the neighbours if she gave her as much as a sniff of information that she could share first-hand.

There were flowers on the table, a large vase of pink and red roses, carnations, and gypsophila.

'Who's brought you those?' she asked.

'They came for you earlier,' Pam said. 'I hope you don't mind but I put them in water. They're beautiful.'

Jess took the card out of its envelope and groaned inwardly.

'Hope you had a great first day. Missing you already. x'

'Who are they from?' Pam hovered around as if she wasn't really that interested but dying to know all the same.

'Work colleagues in Manchester,' Jess fibbed.

'That's nice of them.' Pam flicked on the kettle. 'Cup of tea?'

'Yes, thanks.'

'I thought we might drive out to Ilam this weekend.' Pam popped teabags into two mugs. 'I haven't been there in ages, and—'

'I'll more than likely be working.' Jess nipped that in the bud quickly. If she wasn't in the office, she would be flat hunting.

'No problem. Perhaps we can go the weekend after. I meant to tell you, Michelle Marson from number forty-two has died. She had a heart attack yesterday, while we were out having lunch. Peter from next door found her. Her daughter had to travel from Birmingham to identify her body. Can you remember her, Julie? She's divorced now, with three children. Claiming benefits, idle so-and-so.'

Jess zoned out. That was the problem with having older parents. Her mum had been forty-one when she'd had Jess. She was seventy-six now, her dad had been two years older. Since his death, Pam had been on her own. It was inevitable that she would cling on to her whenever she could, but Jess was too independent.

She drank her tea and said goodnight, going upstairs and straight into the shower. Afterwards, she sat on her bed, her thoughts returning to the flowers. If she had her own place, they would have gone in the bin. Reece Masters had a nerve. How dare he send them to her!

At least she'd blocked his number in her phone so he couldn't contact her about them. Unless he used a burner phone like he'd done several times previously. She never answered numbers she didn't recognise, or caller unknown calls, at all now because of this.

She wasn't going to share her new address with him when she found somewhere to rent either, but all the same, she was certain he'd find her.

He'd threatened her immediately when he'd found out she was transferring to Leek. He'd twisted her arm up her back, enough to cause pain but not injury, and she'd closed her eyes, wishing she could shut out the things he was whispering in her ear. How she was his, how she could never leave him. How he wouldn't allow it.

On her phone, she reread some of the messages he'd sent. She'd kept them all, in case she needed them for evidence in the future.

I will cut out your tongue if you dare say a word.
No one will believe you over me.
You're nothing but a whore. I saw you talking to him, looking at him as if you wanted to screw him.

The man Reece was referring to had been her superintendent. He'd been thanking her for her part in a successful operation.

She lay down on the bed, bringing her knees up to her chest. And she'd thought she was going to be much better off with a police officer? He was never going to leave her alone, was he?

It had seemed the perfect solution to date a cop after having several disastrous relationships. First there had been Karl. They'd been together for four years, two of them living together in Salford. But he worked a nine-to-five job as a marketing executive and would always moan about her irregular hours. When she was on call and a murder came in, he was like a spoiled child. In the end, the relationship petered out. She'd moved out and immediately felt relieved.

Aiden had been next. She'd managed three years with him

until he'd had an affair with a mutual friend. Their betrayal had hurt her deeply, but when he'd used the excuse that she thought more of her job and colleagues than him, it was time to end things.

She'd had a brief fling with a lawyer, too, which was quite nice while it lasted. But it had fizzled out regardless of the job this time. It seemed she was unlucky in love.

But Jess knew there would be someone out there for her. A man who would be proud to be with her because of her job. A man who'd accept that she had an important role to play, often at the drop of a hat. Until then, after the debacle with Reece, she was staying single.

CHAPTER TWENTY

Tuesday

It was half past seven. Marsha had left Phil in bed, so thankfully there hadn't been another showdown. It meant that her head was fully in gear for work.

On the way to the station, she popped into the newsagent's to buy a newspaper. There was a small queue, taking her a couple of minutes to get to the counter.

The woman behind it was in her mid-forties with an unnatural tanned face and bottle-blonde hair tied tightly back in a ponytail. False eyelashes, thick tattooed eyebrows, and plumped-up lips gave her the look of a plastic doll.

'Morning,' she said when Marsha handed her a two-pound coin. 'Terrible business up at Dairy Croft Farm. Have you found those girls yet?'

'We're working on it, Sal.' Marsha waited for her change. 'Have you heard anything?'

'Not yet.' She tapped the side of her nose twice. 'I'll be sure to let you know if I do. How is Mrs Prophet doing?'

'I haven't had an update yet.' Marsha turned away, heading for the door before Sal had the chance to say anything else. She was the best gossip in Leek, but she often went on and on because of it. Still, Marsha knew she'd be in touch if she had information.

She came out of the shop, mobile phone in hand, scanning her emails as she walked, glancing up every now and then to see if she'd be in anyone's way.

A few seconds later, something caught her eye, and she groaned inwardly. Dean Barker was in front of her.

'What do you want?' she snapped.

'Can't a man walk on the pavement without you thinking I'm after a date?' He came closer to her. 'Actually, I did want to see you, though.'

'You'll have to contact me at the station. I'm busy.' She pushed past him and continued on her way. Bloody creep.

'Hey, wait up.' He jogged back to her and grabbed her arm. His smile was all sweetness and light, but she knew it was fake as he dug his fingers into her.

'Dean, we're on a main road, not some dark alley. You need to remember that if you do anything to harm me, you'll be caught on camera, and we'll have you up in court by tomorrow morning.' Marsha's threat was meaningful, her words clear and concise, but inside she was shaking. It was a human reaction, though. She'd met a lot of creeps in her time but none as dangerous.

She pulled her arm away. 'Goodbye, Mr Barker.'

'I'm not done yet.'

'Oh, but I am. You don't intimidate me like you used to.'

Dean laughed heartily.

Marsha remained quiet, a constant stream of traffic passing them on the main road. She stared at him. He was a bad boy, a charmer, but a downright thug when pushed. Yet to look at him, you wouldn't get that impression.

Groomed to perfection, he was slick, in every sense of the word. The shaved head suited him, and the scar underneath his right eye was faded compared to the blue of his irises. His suit was tailored and expensive, his shirt and shoes designer.

'Maybe, maybe not.' Dean glared back. 'But I will be seeing you around, mark my words.'

Marsha rolled her eyes in dramatic fashion. But she knew he deemed her as a threat, or maybe even as a challenge. Would he eventually hurt her, a serving police officer?

'What's your game, Barker?'

'Nothing.' Dean raised his hands in mock surrender and smiled. 'I just like keeping an eye on my favourite inspector.'

She stepped towards him, pointing in his face. 'Stay away from me,' she demanded.

'I'll be seeing you, Marsha Clay.'

She watched him for a few moments, then continued on her way. That bastard. How dare he try to intimidate her. He was the crook. She would never bow down to his threats.

The trouble with working and living in the same area was something Marsha worried about often. Then again, most police officers faced the same predicament. They couldn't get into the station, or out to locations, quickly if they didn't live locally. It was a double-edged sword.

But seeing Barker had brought back memories of things Marsha tried not to think about too much.

Marsha had been sixteen when her eighteen-year-old brother, Joe, had been killed. There had been a fight in a pub, and Joe had intervened, hoping to calm things down. Instead, he'd ended up with a knife wound to his chest.

The first Marsha had known about it was when the police called in the early hours. She'd never forget being told her big brother had been fatally stabbed.

Up until that moment, she hadn't thought of joining the

police force. The original plan had been to go to Staffordshire University to study journalism and media studies.

Career wise, it had sent her in a completely different direction. Seeing so much of what the police did first-hand, over time, made her realise she wanted to do the same, but she didn't do anything about it for a while.

Marsha only had one brother. She became the child who was left behind, the one people talked about. The label of "the girl whose brother was murdered" followed her around. It was inevitable in a small market town, but it weighed her down, too.

Her parents had a rough time afterwards. Her mum blamed her dad, Terry, for letting Joe go out. Terry accused Gina of being too easy on the lad when he was younger. His death changed everything. Nothing was ever the same.

As a teenager, she remembered that no one would come forward about the murder, but soon there were rumours about it being one of the Barker brothers. The Barker family were renowned for their violence and criminal activities. There were three brothers and a sister, all ruling the estate where Marsha used to live.

But gradually, the police on the case got to the bottom of things and people talked. When the trial came round, there were a few witnesses who were intimidated, but the jury convicted Dean Barker of manslaughter, much to his family's anger. He was nineteen.

At least he got to that age.

Once he'd been put away for seven years, hardly long enough in their eyes, for a time they were able to get on with their lives. But when Dean was released from prison, the harassment started.

It was his release that made Marsha more determined to join the police. She wanted to convict families like the Barkers, who thought they were above the law.

As soon as she hit the streets as a police constable in uniform, the Barkers came for her at every opportunity. Harry Barker, the patriarch of the family, wanted to pay her to be an informant for him, and when she refused, he said he'd make her pay in different ways.

It wasn't until he was put away the year after for armed robbery that things got better. But each year, one or other of the Barkers got on her case. If they weren't asking her to do things for them, in return for cash, they were wanting her help to get someone off the hook.

She never worked with them, no matter how threatening they became.

Over time, as a new generation of Barkers grew up, some tried to wheedle their way in again, but more often than not, they lived side by side, tolerating each other. It was only Dean who appeared like a bad penny every now and then, like now.

And, like today, she always wondered what his reasoning was behind it.

CHAPTER TWENTY-ONE

Marsha arrived at work extremely rattled by bumping into Dean Barker. But she gave him no more of her time once she switched her computer on.

Now, she was busy checking through what had come in overnight. There had been no sightings of Tamara or Maisie Prophet, which meant they'd been missing for nearly twenty-four hours.

Every available officer was on the case, and others had been drafted in from nearby stations.

The search teams would be starting up again soon, and she was hoping the public who wanted to join in would help rather than hinder. There were a lot of fields belonging to different properties around Dairy Croft Farm, but people needed to be mindful the police had work to do.

She picked up her phone and rang the hospital.

'This is Detective Inspector Clay, Staffordshire Police. Could I have an update on Sylvia Prophet, please?'

'One moment, I'll put you through.'

Marsha searched out a chocolate biscuit from her drawer, relishing the sweet taste of it on her tongue.

'Sister Ashwood speaking.'

Caught out, Marsha swallowed quickly and repeated her query.

'She's stable at the moment, woke up around five a.m.'

'Am I able to see her later this morning? The family will be coming, too, but I need to ask her a few questions.'

'Yes, that will be fine. Her son and daughter-in-law were allowed a quick visit around eleven last night. She's been told her husband has died.'

'Ah, right. I assume she knows her grandchildren are missing, too?'

'I don't think so. Her son wasn't with her long. I expect he didn't want to upset her too much after what she'd been through. It's a terrible shock. Is there any news on the missing girls?'

'We're looking into all leads at the moment.' It was the standard line for every inquiry.

Marsha ended the call shortly afterwards. Poor Mrs Prophet. She had her own injuries and the death of her husband to deal with, never mind her missing grandchildren. Hopefully, there would be news of them today.

Next, she checked over the team's actions for the morning. Jess and Nathan were visiting Prophet and Son and, once she'd had a word with Connor and Emma, she was going to be leaving for the mortuary. John Prophet would get a formal identification, and then she'd go with Dan and Lucy to the hospital. Perhaps she'd learn more about what had happened then.

Emma arrived first, plonking her bag on her desk before sitting down. 'Morning, another grand day,' she shouted through to Marsha. 'Drink?'

'Please. I'm gasping.' Marsha held up her mug, and Emma came to collect it. 'How are you doing?'

'I'm okay.' Emma sighed. 'I went straight into Tilly's room

when I got home, just to see if she was still awake. She was, although she shouldn't have been. I needed to give her a big cuddle. I can't imagine what the Prophets are going through. I wouldn't know what to do with myself, if it were me.'

'Me neither.' Marsha shook her head. 'If the girls haven't been taken, they can't have gone far.'

'Do you think they've left the area?'

Marsha grimaced. 'It's unusual that there's been no sightings of them. Fingers crossed for good news. Then we can get on with everything else.'

'Morning, ladies.' Connor came in and stood in the doorway. He smothered a yawn and then smiled. 'Sorry, found it hard to drop off last night. It was so hot, I had to sleep starkers, and even then I was still sweating.'

'Euw, my eyes.' Emma screwed up her face.

'Yeah, not something I want to imagine either.' Marsha grinned.

'You don't know what you're missing.' Connor laughed. 'Nathan not in yet?'

'He and Jess have gone straight to Prophet and Son to talk to the staff. The garage has reopened today.'

'Oh, yeah. I forgot.'

'What did you two think of Jess yesterday?'

'She's nice,' Emma commented. 'Although what a day to arrive.'

'I liked her, too,' Connor added. 'She seems like she'll fit in well with us riffraff.'

Marsha handed him a piece of paper. 'There's been a hit-and-run come in overnight. Can you visit the scene and the family to get details? It needs to be prioritised and investigated alongside what we're doing now. Plus there will be another family grieving.'

'Will do, boss.' He took the note from her. 'How's Tilly, Emma?'

'She's good, ta. Coffee?'

'Thought you'd never ask.'

Marsha smiled at her officers as they left the room, continuing with their chat. Connor had taken Emma under his wing when she'd joined them. It was nice to see his concern for his work colleague. Connor had children. It must be hard for him, too.

Every officer had their fair share of problems at home, but mostly, like Marsha had earlier, they left them at the door when they arrived at work. She made a mental note to have a quiet word with each of the team, to see if they were coping. Missing children could really take a toll on mental health.

Though she missed Dave dearly, she was lucky to have such a good bunch to work with. She only hoped there weren't going to be problems between Nathan and Jess. Nathan had snapped uncharacteristically yesterday.

Maybe it was a case of the dynamics in the team changing. He was used to going out with Connor all the time. She'd keep an eye on that, too.

For now, it was back to work.

CHAPTER TWENTY-TWO

Nathan was waiting for Jess in the staff car park. He was about to send her a message asking how long she'd be when he saw her parking up. She got out of her car and walked across to him.

She was a nice-looking woman, slim with short red hair. She wore navy trousers and a matching waistcoat, a short-sleeved white shirt, and large sunglasses. A leather handbag had been placed across her body.

She got into the passenger seat of his car. 'Hi, sorry I'm a few minutes late. Can't judge the traffic yet. Have you been waiting long?'

'Long enough.' Nathan gave a faint smile, and they set off. Then, deciding to at least try and be civil rather than cause an atmosphere, he gave her some background about the garage.

'Prophet and Son has been going since nineteen eighty-two,' he told her, indicating to pull out onto the main road. 'I think everyone in Leek will know of it. Most of the force get their cars serviced there as they're so reliable, and they'll always fit you in if there's a problem. It's just through the traffic lights on the Buxton Road, do you know it?'

'I can't remember it,' Jess said. 'Is it far?'

'Only a few minutes.' Nathan turned up the radio as a song came on. 'I haven't heard this in ages.'

'Me neither.' Jess sang along to the lyrics.

Nathan did the same, catching Jess's eyes.

'I wouldn't have had you down as a Katy Perry fan,' she teased.

'Are you kidding? I've loved her since I first set eyes on her.'

'You would have been fifteen, at a guess, when that song came out?'

'Seventeen. I'm thirty-two.'

'Ah, I'm thirty-five.'

They sang quietly together again. Nathan drove through the lights, and Prophet and Son came up on their right. The property was at the end of a row of terraced houses and was a long, single-storey building. In front, leading onto the main road was the forecourt. On one side there were vehicles for sale: on the other, a queue for the service department.

'Do you have kids, Nathan?' Jess asked after they parked up.

'Yes.' Nathan took out a photo from his wallet and showed it to her.

Jess saw a young girl who was the image of her father, with big brown eyes, dark hair to her shoulders with a fringe, and a huge beam on her face. Her stomach flipped.

'She's gorgeous,' she said.

'Takes after her father.' He chuckled. It morphed into a grimace, but he didn't elaborate. In fact, he seemed upset about something.

'I'd love to have children one day, if I can ever find the right man to settle down with. Have you been married long?'

'Seven years.' Nathan opened the door to signal that the conversation was over.

'I see trade hasn't been affected,' she changed the subject, releasing her seatbelt.

'Maybe that was because they were closed yesterday.' Nathan reached for a pair of gloves from the side door. 'Do you need any?'

'Got some, thanks.'

Inside, they introduced themselves and then separated to talk to people. While Jess was shown to the office, Nathan went to the repairs section.

There were several people, working in different bays. A Renault Clio had been lifted, and a teenage girl was being shown what to look for underneath it by a man in his thirties. Another mechanic had a car revving up, attached to a computer.

Chris Osbourne, the maintenance manager, spotted Nathan, wiped his hands on a rag, and came over.

Nathan shook hands with him, having known him for quite some years. 'Sorry about what's happened.'

'I still can't believe it. I bet you got a shock when you saw him, too.'

Nathan nodded but said nothing else.

'Any news of the girls yet?'

'We have several lines of enquiry open. There's a search team out again this morning.'

They stepped inside an office at the back. Chris closed the door, the noise fading a little.

The room was a tip, with files and paperwork stacked precariously wherever there was a spare space, and sometimes where there wasn't.

Chris sat down at a desk, pointing to a chair on the opposite side.

'We're just asking questions to people in general at the

moment.' Nathan removed a log book manual off the seat and sat down. 'Have you noticed anything unusual, had trouble with anyone lately?'

Chris sat quietly for a moment, then shook his head. 'We were sent home yesterday when Dan called us, but we all ended up at the pub. We were talking these kinds of things through, and we drew a blank. There's been nothing happening. Not for a long time, really.'

'How long have you worked here now?'

'Twenty-three years, since I was sixteen. Me and Dan left school on Friday and started here full-time on the Monday. I used to work Saturdays before that, Dan, too. We've been good friends since junior school.'

'So you'll know if there are any long-time feuds or problems with anyone?'

'Yes, but there weren't. I think the only fallings-out are with the staff every now and then. If we get a lad who doesn't fit in, that kind of thing.'

'That happen lately?'

'Not as far as anyone can remember.' He ran a hand through thick, greying hair. 'We're genuinely flummoxed, especially someone going to his home. Dan rang and said Sylvia was stable. That's good.'

Nathan nodded. 'I'm going to have a quick chat with some of the lads, and then I'll be on my way. Unless you have anything further to add?'

'No.' Chris looked on sheepishly. 'Nothing at all.'

Gut feeling, Nathan wasn't quite sure he was telling him everything.

CHAPTER TWENTY-THREE

Jess was introduced to the office manager, Sarah Cradford. She was a thin woman, with long blonde hair in a messy updo that suited the hippy-style, floral dress and wedge heels she was wearing.

Sarah told Jess that she'd been working there almost as long as the business was established and was due to retire the next year.

Jess followed her through a side door, along a corridor and into a room where there were six desks and a small office crammed into almost as little a space as their team had at the station. The heads of several women and two men bobbed up over computer monitors, and she gave them a friendly smile.

'Through here,' Sarah said. 'You can use Lucy's office.'

'Is she here full-time?'

'Not quite. She works school hours, Monday through Friday, and only during term times.'

'Do you get on well?'

'Yes, she's okay.'

'And she was having a day off yesterday?' Jess asked.

'Training day at school, so she was taking the girls out, I

think. They often come into the office, though. It's nice, we know them well.' She rubbed a hand over her chin. 'We're all so worried.'

'Are the family close?' Jess glanced around, spotting nothing out of the ordinary.

'Yes. We all are, really. Because it's a family run business, the Prophets looked after us well.'

'There aren't any secrets, rumours, that kind of thing?'

Sarah shook her head. Suddenly, she burst into tears. 'It's such a shock to us all. Who would do such a thing?'

'We're working on finding out,' Jess assured her. 'I'll have a quick word with the staff in general, and then I'll leave you be. Once again, I'm sorry for your loss.'

Jess had a chat with the staff sitting at their desks. It all seemed above board, and she didn't pick up on anything. People seemed genuinely shocked at the news.

Afterwards, she was walking along the corridor back to the reception area to wait for Nathan, when she was called back by Sarah.

'You mentioned secrets earlier,' she told her. 'I hate talking out of turn, but thinking about it now, it could be something you need to know. When John Prophet retired, there was talk about Dan taking over the business for him. And, to all intents and purposes, he has. But Dan has been really stressed lately.'

'You saw signs of this?'

'A lot of the staff come to me with their problems.' Sarah placed a hand on her chest and smiled. 'I suppose I'm a motherly figure to them all. But this time, I asked Dan if he was okay, and he told me what had been happening.'

A door along the corridor opened, and a woman came towards them. She smiled before disappearing into the toilets.

Sarah moved closer to Jess and lowered her voice. 'Dan told me that his father hadn't signed the business over to him like everyone thought. John was a bit of a taskmaster, some might say a bully, but he got things done. He'd told Dan he had to prove he was good enough to inherit the business by running it alone for a year before it would be his. And even then, he was planning on keeping a majority share of the company.'

'How did Dan take that?' Jess queried.

'In his stride, I thought, once I knew what was going on. It was really nasty of John to do that to him. Dan has given his life to this business, and he's good at what he does. But he was often ridiculed by John in front of everyone. John would always call him out, saying he was useless. It wasn't nice at times, to be honest.'

Jess waited, but there was nothing more forthcoming. Sarah was glancing along the corridor again.

'Thanks for that information,' Jess said. 'I'm glad Dan has you to look out for him.'

Sarah nodded and then left.

Jess suspected she wanted to be gone before the woman came out of the toilets, so it didn't seem as if she'd been telling tales. But the information she'd given her could be useful.

Finally in the reception area, Jess waited for Nathan. It was a pleasant area for customers, with lots of bright colours, a drinks machine and numerous plants.

On the wall were several framed certificates. At the far end was a newspaper clipping with a photo of Mr Prophet and Dan, along with three other men. They were leaning against a truck, thumbs up, posing for the image taken outside the garage.

There was also a framed photo of John Prophet with Marsha, being handed a certificate. Jess recalled something

Marsha had said the day before. That could have been taken when she'd last seen him.

Finally, Nathan rejoined her, and they went back to his car.

'Did you find out anything?' she asked him.

'Nothing, which is good because we weren't really looking for anything.'

'It could be anyone at the moment.'

'It won't be someone working here. I've known most of them for years.'

'And people snap in seconds, sometimes over the silliest of things.'

Nathan shook his head and stormed off to his car.

Jess frowned. Assume nothing, believe nobody, check everything? Weren't they supposed to keep an open mind?

In the car, she told him what she'd found out from Sarah. He appeared a bit shamefaced then. Served him right for not listening to her before snapping.

'That's interesting,' he commented. 'Dan Prophet might well have an alibi, but he could have paid someone to do his dirty work if he was angry with his father.'

'You mean because he didn't mention it, he could be covering something up?'

'It's possible.' Nathan checked his phone. 'I've got a message from Marsha. She wants us to go to The Station to speak to the manager. He says he has some CCTV footage we need to see from Sunday. It seems Dan and John Prophet were having an argument, which he's caught on camera. Plus he wants a chat with us.'

'That's my neck of the woods, although I lived on the opposite side of the main road.'

'What about now, Jess?' Nathan pulled away from the forecourt. 'What's brought you to Leek?'

'My dad died, so I thought it best to be nearer to home.'

'Ah, sorry to hear that.'

'Thanks. My mum still lives in Rushton Spencer.'

She turned her face to the window, hoping he wouldn't see her blushing. It was a little economical with the truth, but she could live with that.

She saw the sign to Rudyard pass on her left.

'I haven't been to Rudyard since my teens,' she said. 'I used to love going out on the lake.'

'The Blackpool of the Potteries?'

'What?' She turned to him in curiosity.

'That's what it was known as. They have over five hundred thousand visitors a year now.'

'Wow, I had no idea. All I can remember is walking by the lake, having ice cream, and riding on the small train. I'll have to visit on a day off.'

'Yeah, I should come more often, but it's the same old, same old. You always forget things on your doorstep. Still, when you do visit, watch out for the bare necessities.' Nathan said, deadpan.

Jess laughed at his reference to *The Jungle Book*, written by Rudyard Kipling and adapted for the big screen. They seemed to be on an even keel again now, much better than the snappy man he was earlier.

A few miles along, Nathan turned left into Station Road and again into the car park of The Station. He parked and switched off the engine.

'Let's go see what Dan and his dad were up to on Sunday.'

CHAPTER TWENTY-FOUR

Before going to see the family of the hit-and-run victim, Connor had spent an hour at the scene of the crime. He always felt it necessary to see everything first-hand, so he could get a feel of what had gone on.

The accident report said that the car skittled the victim as he'd been crossing the road. It was a side street, not a main thoroughfare, and wouldn't have been busy at that time of night. There were no streetlights out either, to hinder a driver's visibility.

Residents had come out when they'd heard the noise, but no one had seen the vehicle. One of the main reasons for leaving the scene of a crime was because someone was intoxicated. The driver would go home, sleep it off and, in some instances, report the car stolen the next morning. Even if they didn't ring the police, cars never hid damage that had been done, so they'd figure it out eventually and arrest the suspect that way.

Sometimes it was joyriders, or TWOCs, taken without consent. He recalled a case from a couple of years ago when a twelve-year-old boy had fatally mown down a woman in her sixties after taking his parents' brand-new BMW out while they were asleep. The lad had come away with three years' detention. Connor had cited it as an example in many school talks since, still unable to believe the lad's actions had caused so much grief.

Connor had asked uniformed officers to get any dashcam or doorbell camera footage to see what they could pull up about the accident. A link of one had been sent to his phone, but he couldn't make out much more than the side of a small white vehicle. Once he'd seen enough, he went to the address he'd been given for the victim.

Western Street was a long road with houses numbered up to the two hundreds and a mixed bunch of property types. Terraced houses, semi-detached, and a few larger homes.

He gathered his folder and walked up the path of number seventeen, acknowledging the neighbour out in the garden next door. This house was a pre-war detached, with an arched brick porch, and a welcoming red front door. Two cars were parked in front of a double garage.

He rang the doorbell. The incident had happened late last night, so he wasn't sure who the family liaison officer would be, or if one had been allocated yet.

A man in his late sixties opened the door. He was bald, his head covered in age spots, wearing thick-rimmed black glasses. He seemed exhausted, no doubt from lack of sleep as well as grief.

Connor held up his warrant card. 'Mr Adams? I'm Detective Constable Wilson, Connor. I believe you're expecting me.'

'Yes, come through.'

He was shown into a living room, two of the original rooms knocked into one. It was full of flowery soft furnishings, sun streaming in through double glass doors, which led onto a small conservatory.

A woman was sitting on the settee and stood up when she saw him. A similar age to the man, she was petite with a short, grey bob. Her eyes were red and puffy, her hands shaking as she scrunched up a tissue.

'This is Connor,' Mr Adams said. 'He's come to take down some details.'

'Mrs Adams, I'm so sorry for your loss.'

'Please call me Joan, and this is Gerald. Sit down. Can I get you a drink?'

'No, I'm fine, thank you.' Connor opened his folder and pulled out his iPad. 'I know you will have spoken to the police last night, but I wanted to get the details down in full, so we can start to investigate what happened while we're collecting evidence.'

Joan let out a sob. Gerald moved to sit next to her and took her hand in his own.

'Nick and his wife have separated,' he said. 'He's been living here for about four months now. They're going through a divorce. Well, they were.'

Connor typed out the details. 'Was the breakup amicable?' he asked next.

'It was hard on him,' Joan said, sniffing. 'He took it badly. She just fell out of love with him. There was no one else involved. Not that we know of anyway.'

'Any children?'

'Two. Patrick is nineteen, and Mabel is fifteen. He saw them most weekends, whenever they weren't out with friends. They grow up so quickly.'

Connor nodded his sympathies. He pointed to a photo. 'Is that Nicholas?'

'Nick, yes.' Gerald got up to retrieve it and handed it to Connor. 'He was a good boy, our lad.'

Nick looked very much like his father. He was fishing by the side of a lake. Smiling as he raised a can of drink, his legs stretched out in a relaxed pose. His happiness made Connor sad, knowing Nick was no longer able to enjoy his life through no fault of his own.

'So last night, was he out late for a reason?' he continued.

'He'd left work early after the dreadful news of John Prophet and his family. We can't believe what's happened. Have you found those two little girls yet?'

'No, sir, but we are doing everything we can.' Connor's brain was ticking over. He typed out some thoughts and then continued with his conversation. 'Can you talk me through what happened last night? What time did Nick get in, and then go out again, or hadn't he come home at all until the incident?'

'He'd gone to work as normal, but when Dan rang to tell everyone what had happened, the garage was closed for the day. Nick rang us then, and said he was spending the rest of the day with his colleagues. I don't think he knew what to do really.'

Connor stopped typing. 'Nick worked at Prophet and Son?'

'Yes. He was a mechanic, been there since he was eighteen.'

Connor was quite good at keeping his face straight in situations like this. He'd had years to practice. But a murder in the morning, and a hit-and-run the same evening, with a connection, had him struggling to keep a frown from appearing.

He listened as Gerald went on. 'He came in around four p.m. He sat with us for a while, had some tea, and then he went out again.'

'Did he say where he was going?'

'He walked to the pub, The Traveller's Rest at the end of the street.' Joan shook her head. 'He was really upset and said he needed to be alone.'

'May I take this photo with me, please?' Connor held it up. 'I promise to take good care of it and get it back to you as soon as I can.'

'Yes, of course. Anything we can do to help.'

'Thank you. I'll keep in touch, and there will be a family liaison officer coming to you shortly. They'll arrange for you to identify the body. They'll be your first point of contact, but you can call me anytime.' He gave them a card with his details on it. 'Once again, I'm so sorry for your loss.'

Back in his car, Connor went over his notes, making sure he hadn't missed anything. He'd have to get them back to be signed. But, for now, his thoughts were on another thing.

Was it a coincidence that two men linked to Prophet and Son were now dead, and that neither had been an accident? And with Tamara and Maisie still missing, and the garage now run by Dan, was someone hellbent on revenge?

Was it possible they had a serial killer on the loose?

CHAPTER TWENTY-FIVE

After a quick update with the DCI, Marsha made a quick call to Dan and Lucy Prophet. Ryan had suggested she do a brief press conference with them that morning, and she wanted to know if they were up to it. They'd agreed, and it was being set up once they'd identified John Prophet's body.

The mortuary was on the edge of Leek, and the single-storey building always reminded Marsha of a Portacabin from the front until she got inside. From there, it opened up into a large area, modernised throughout, and extended back a long way to reveal several further rooms and labs.

She met Dan and Lucy Prophet in the foyer, next to the viewing room. The couple looked dreadful, and who could blame them? She imagined they'd barely had any sleep. Their daughters were still missing, and as well, they had a harrowing morning ahead of them.

At times like this, Marsha always felt so inadequate, but they had a whole force searching for Tamara and Maisie, and the person who had murdered Dan's father and attacked his mother.

PC Joy was with them and, after a quick update with her,

Marsha checked to see if both Dan and Lucy wanted to identify John, or as it was Dan's father, if he preferred to go in alone.

'We're doing it together,' Dan replied. 'We've spoken about it earlier.'

Marsha nodded. 'Let's go through.'

The viewing room was small, but there was another room off it. Almost the length of the wall was a pane of glass at waist height. On the other side was a body lying on a table, completely covered in a white sheet, and a technician waiting to reveal the victim's face.

At Marsha's acknowledgement, the sheet was pulled back.

Dan gave out a strangled sob. Lucy burst into tears and sank into his chest. Their pain was raw, but Marsha still had to ask for confirmation.

'Is this your dad, Dan?' Marsha said softly.

'Yes, it is.'

It was over in seconds, but they wanted a few minutes on their own. Truth be told, Marsha was relieved to leave them to it. It was one of the worst parts of her job, relatives' grief often seeping under her skin. But it was a vital part of any investigation.

She and Rachel waited in the foyer. They sat side by side on a small settee, neither of them feeling the need to make small talk.

It was several minutes before Dan and Lucy emerged.

'Are you okay?' Marsha asked, knowing that the question was a rhetorical one.

Dan nodded, Lucy in his arms.

'We can head to the station when you're ready. And then we can go to the hospital. I believe you saw your mum last night?'

'We didn't get to speak to her much because it was late. But she was distressed and asking for Dad, and I...' Dan struggled with his words. 'I told her before she heard it from anyone else.'

'I know, I rang earlier to check how she was doing. How did she take it?'

'I'm not sure it sank in. She did cry a little, though.'

'Did you ask her about yesterday?'

Dan shook his head. 'I thought I'd leave that to you.'

'Okay, thanks. Do you need some time before we leave? Perhaps grab a coffee on the way, or something?'

'No, thanks. We want to do the press conference as quickly as possible.'

Half an hour later, Marsha was sitting at the front of the press room, this time facing the media. The weather was still stuffy, which was good for her because she definitely had sweat patches under her arms due to stress.

By her side were Dan and Lucy Prophet. They were each holding one of the teddy bears Marsha had seen in the children's rooms. It was so poignant, and Marsha had to push down her emotion.

She swallowed her nerves, cleared her throat, and addressed the crowd with an update of how the case was coming on. Luckily, she knew most of the people she was looking at, so she focussed on them instead of thinking of how many viewers the broadcast would be going out to live.

'I'd like to ask Tamara and Maisie's parents to say a few words now,' she finished, indicating to Dan that he could start.

Dan sat forward slightly, put the bear he was holding on the table, picked up the prepared statement, and began to read.

'Tamara and Maisie have been missing since yesterday morning. We are appealing to anyone who may have seen them to come forward and let us know.' Lucy held up an image of the two girls. 'We miss them very much. Maisie is only four, and even though we know her big sister will be taking care of her, we just want them home.'

A flurry of lights flashed at them as he continued to read the statement. Once he was finished, Marsha felt drained but had to finish with some words of her own.

'Police teams are still actively searching for the missing girls, and details are being shared on social media wherever possible. If anyone knows the whereabouts of Tamara and Maisie, please ring us on the helpline, the number of which will be coming across the bottom of your screen. Anything, no matter how small, could be a great help in our investigation. Thank you.'

Answering no questions, Marsha ushered them out of the room and into another until the press had left.

Her heart went out to the couple as she watched them sitting in a dazed silence. What a morning they'd been through, and yet she assumed every hour so far would have felt like it stretched ahead of them like a week until there was news.

She couldn't begin to imagine how they were feeling. Her own family was safe. How could she possibly know?

CHAPTER TWENTY-SIX

Due to the nature of the admission, Sylvia Prophet was in a side room in the hospital. Marsha stayed back from the bed while Dan and Lucy comforted her. Then she pulled up a chair and sat down.

'Hello again,' Sylvia said.

'Hello, Sylvia,' Marsha replied, glad she seemed to recognise who she was. 'How are you feeling today?'

'I'm in a lot of pain, but I'm, well, I'm lucky to be here, I think.'

'I can't begin to tell you how sorry I am for what's happened, but we will be working flat out on this case until we find out who did this to you and John. And we're searching for Tamara and Maisie, too.'

'Thank you.' Sylvia's voice held a slight tremor in it.

'Are you able to tell me what happened yesterday? Anything, no matter how small, may be useful to us.'

'I'll try and remember as much as I can. I'd just made breakfast. The children were singing with John. There was so much laughter mixed in with it. John was making up silly words and saying they were singing the wrong lyrics. It was some sort of rapper song. Tamara knew all the words, and Maisie the dance moves. It's a memory I'll cherish now.'

A tear rolled down Sylvia's cheek.

'I suppose we didn't hear much outside because of the noise. We lost Rollo, our collie, last month. He would have heard someone approaching, if he was in a vehicle.' She frowned. 'Did he come on foot, the man?'

Marsha sat forward. 'You got a good look at him?'

'It's a bit vague. The doorbell rang, and John went to answer it. He was still singing as he left the room. Then I heard voices, and they were getting louder. I went to see what was going on, and he... he, the man, was stabbing John in the stomach.'

'Oh, Mum.' Dan reached for Sylvia's arm, his words choked.

Sylvia patted the top of his hand before continuing, turning back to face Marsha.

'I don't know what came over me, but I flew at him. He wasn't going to hurt my John. But when I got close enough, he hit out and I fell backwards into the wall. I can't remember anything after that.' She glanced at Dan and Lucy. 'I'm glad, really. I couldn't live that nightmare over and over.'

'Sylvia,' Marsha said. 'Did you know the man?'

'No, I'd never seen him before,' Sylvia replied, 'When I'd regained consciousness, he'd gone, and I saw...' She covered her mouth for a moment. 'I saw John, lying there. I managed to drag myself to the phone to get help.'

'Can you describe him?'

'White, about forty, a bit untidy, with stubble. He had short greasy hair. I think it was brown.'

'What was he wearing?'

'Jeans, I think, and a dark blue T-shirt. He had work boots on, too.'

'You're doing great,' Marsha encouraged. 'Was he taller than John?'

'Yes, but not much.' Sylvia shuddered. 'He had deep blue eyes. I'll never forget those.'

'And you didn't see a vehicle through the open door?'

'No, it all happened so quickly. I'm so sorry.'

'*I'm* sorry to rake it all up again for you. Thank you, Sylvia. You've been very brave.'

Marsha was about to stand up when Sylvia grasped her hand.

'He's taken our girls, hasn't he? That's what he really came for, and John wouldn't let him in.'

'We don't know,' Marsha said truthfully. She noticed that Lucy was crying quietly. 'We're still hoping they're hiding somewhere, but it's been a while now. I'm sorry I can't tell you more.'

Dan followed Marsha when she left to rejoin Rachel in the corridor. 'Can I go there, yet, to the farm?' he asked. 'I could help with the search.'

'I don't think the property will have been cleared for forensics yet,' Marsha explained.

'But I can stay out in the fields, can't I?'

'They've been searched several times now, and I don't think—'

'I have to do *something*. I can't just sit around and wait.'

Marsha sensed his frustration. But she didn't want him to see anything that he'd remember later, that would come back to haunt his dreams. Most of their work had been done, but who knew what might trigger something for him, something that they wouldn't think about until it was too late.

'I can't promise, but I'll make some calls,' she said. 'I won't be a minute.'

Marsha left him with Rachel while she moved to one side to contact Pete Draycott, the Crime Scene Manager. She'd worked with him for over ten years, and she would do whatever he said was necessary.

'I think it will be fine for him to come this afternoon,' he told her. 'We can't let him into the house. The crime scene needs to be cleaned, but he could look around the garden and fields at the back.'

'Thanks. I expect he only wants to know we're doing a thorough job and will be satisfied once he's seen for himself.'

'Understood. He must be at his wit's end. It's not hopeful for the girls, is it?'

Marsha ran a hand through her hair. 'I'm trying not to think about that.'

There was a pause as they both drifted off with their own thoughts, then he spoke again. 'I'll alert the team who are still there.'

'Cheers, Pete.'

When Marsha got in her car again, she blew out a lengthy breath. What the Prophet family must be going through at the moment was beyond her comprehension.

She checked her phone to see if anyone had been trying to contact her while it had been switched to silent. There was a message from Connor, asking her to call him.

He answered after two rings.

'You'll never guess where the hit-and-run victim works, boss?' he spoke first, before she had the chance. 'He was a mechanic at Prophet and Son.'

'No way!' Marsha was shocked.

'Yes, way.'

'Well, of course. I didn't mean... anyway, that can't be a coincidence. Where are you?'

'Just parked up at the station.'

She checked her watch to see it was nearly one o'clock. 'Nip upstairs to see if the others are back, and if they haven't had anything to eat, grab some sandwiches. We'll have a working lunch. My shout.'

'Cheers, boss. Cheese and onion for you?'

'Yes, and cakes. Not from the canteen, though. Fetch some fresh ones. A vanilla slice for me.'

Marsha disconnected the call and sat for a moment. What was going on? Now they had a murder, a hit-and-run death, an assault, and two little girls missing.

And, once Nicholas Adams had been formally identified later that day, how on earth were Dan and Lucy Prophet going to feel about that news?

One thing was certain, someone seemed to be coming after the Prophet family.

CHAPTER TWENTY-SEVEN

Back at the station, Marsha took the opportunity to nip to the loo before getting bombarded by her team. Her phone rang while she was there. Unable to take the call, she heard a message come in shortly afterwards. Once she'd washed her hands, she retrieved it.

We still need to talk. When will you be home tonight?

Marsha sighed. Phil knew full well she was in the middle of a case, so it would be long hours until it was solved. Was this his way of getting her to say she couldn't spare the time, and then put the blame on her for never being available? She sent a message back to see.

Not sure. Major developments, so I doubt I'll be home early

Well, when can we talk then? I need to know.

What's so important it can't wait?

No reply.

She waited for a minute, then cursed under her breath She could do without his games right now.

She walked into the office, immediately spotting someone who always brightened up her day. Finn Lockley, Senior

Crime Scene Investigator, was talking to the team, a mug of coffee already in his hand.

Finn was forty-two, short brown hair and healthy looking in a way that Marsha envied. Fresh faced, sometimes wearing glasses but not today. He seemed to be able to eat whatever he wanted and never put on weight, whereas she only had to sniff a cake and it went straight on her hips.

Still, it would never stop her tucking into the sweet stuff. For the most part, she kept herself fit walking Larry, working out in the gym downstairs at the station, and chasing the odd criminal. It would have to do.

'Well, aren't you a sight for sore eyes?' she teased. 'Brought any doughnuts?'

'Totally slipped my mind.' Finn laughed and pointed to the door. 'I can always go and fetch some.'

'No need. An IOU will be written out for you, though. Lucky for you, I have a vanilla slice.' She picked up her food. 'You got something for us?'

Finn held up a manila file. 'I have.'

Marsha glanced at Emma. 'Anything come in that I should know about?'

'Update from the search about an hour ago, boss.' Emma shook her head. 'No sightings.'

'Where *are* they?' Marsha groaned. 'What about the people we want to talk to?'

'Still working on it. I haven't spotted a white van on CCTV around Dairy Croft Farm, but I still have a lot to view.'

'Thanks.' Marsha beckoned to Finn. 'Come on through to my lair.'

Finn sat across from her. He wasn't a local, but through work they had known each other for years. He was raised in Stoke-on-Trent and lived in Rudyard now, in a house at the side of the lake that he'd been renovating for a few years.

Marsha had never visited, but the photos he'd shown them as and when he'd finished a room were out of this world.

'Not much to go on, I'm afraid.' Finn put down his coffee mug and handed her the file. 'There are no prints anywhere of anyone else in the house. No footprints as the ground was so dry. No tyre marks for a vehicle either, for the same reason.'

'That's not helpful, Finn.' Marsha took it from him and scanned it quickly. She looked up with a frown.

'Don't shoot the messenger.' He raised his hands in mock surrender.

'I've also had a pathology report from Ruby. John Prophet died from multiple stab wounds, and one in particular punctured his heart. He would have died within minutes. So, there is nothing to go on.' Marsha groaned, placing her head on the desk momentarily. 'Thanks for bringing them, though.'

'No problem. I was on my way past.'

Marsha knew that was probably a fib. Finn's office was on the other side of Leek, and Rudyard was in the opposite direction. She liked to think that he'd popped in specially to see her. Even if it wasn't true, she enjoyed seeing him. They had a good rapport.

It made her remember the times when she and Phil had made each other laugh. Sadly, she had a feeling that might never happen again.

Jess was in a world of her own when Emma spoke to her.

'Have you got a partner, Jess?' she asked.

'No, I'm in between arseholes at the moment, thank goodness.' She paused. 'Sorry, that was a bit harsh.'

Emma laughed. 'Unlucky in love?'

'You could say that.'

'At least you don't have to listen to someone snoring next to you all night.' Emma rolled her eyes. 'My fella, Josh, sounds like the London Underground at times when I stay over. I swear there might be a murder soon.' She coloured. 'Oh, that was in bad taste, I'm sorry now!'

'No worries.' Jess smiled to show she understood it was a joke.

'You don't have any hobbies or things we need to be worried about, Jess?' Connor joined in. 'Like turning into a vampire after dark?'

'I'll let you know once dusk sets in,' Jess toyed with him. 'Just be sure not to show me your neck.'

'Well, that rules you out then.' Nathan twanged an elastic band at Connor, narrowly missing his nose. 'Who'd want to bite your skin when you only wash once in a blue moon?'

'Cheeky git. I'll have you know it's at least once a week.' He sniffed his armpits. 'Mind, in this heat, it's more like twice a day.'

Emma got out some body spray and squirted it around the room liberally, much to the men's dismay.

'It smells like a flower shop,' Nathan protested as Connor feigned a coughing fit.

Jess was watching Marsha in her office. The blinds were open so, from where she was sitting, she could see straight in. Marsha and Finn laughed at something she'd said, then their heads went down to look at a file. A bit of grimacing, and then more laughter.

A few minutes passed, and they were still talking. Before the next briefing, she needed a trip to the ladies. Sidling past Emma, she leaned in conspiratorially.

'Can I ask you something?'

'Sure.'

'Marsha and Finn. They seem a bit... friendly,' she whispered.

Emma nodded. 'They get on really well. It's a shame Marsha is happily married, because I think they'd make a great couple. And it's clear to everyone that Finn only has eyes for Miss Marsha.'

'Oh?' Jess was intrigued.

Marsha's door opened, and she and Finn reappeared.

Jess shot out of the room, as if she were a child being caught doing something naughty. When she came back, Finn had gone and Marsha was perched on the end of the spare desk, waiting for her to return.

'Catch-up time. I'll start with the forensic results.' Marsha held up the file and went through everything she'd discussed with Finn. 'So, where do we go from here?'

CHAPTER TWENTY-EIGHT

Nathan gave an update of the visit to Prophet and Son and then showed footage of the CCTV clip he'd had emailed to him since talking to the landlord at The Station. They gathered round to view it.

John and Dan Prophet were in a corridor away from the bar, after emerging from the gents. John grabbed Dan's arm as he walked off. He pointed his finger in his son's face, angry about something.

Dan tried to leave, but again, John pulled him back. A few seconds of a heated conversation, and this time John stormed off, leaving Dan to pace the corridor, before following him.

'The landlord said he'd noticed them arguing but at the time didn't think anything of it,' Nathan added. 'He said they seemed to settle again once back at their table. But he did mention that John was a regular there and known for his arrogance and hot-headed temper.'

'Great work,' Marsha said. 'You, too, Jess. We'll have a word with Dan as to why he didn't mention they'd had a fall out.'

'I'm not sure if it seems too squeaky clean at Prophet and

Son, or if everyone is happy, boss,' Jess said. 'I mean, other than what Sarah Cradford told me, there wasn't any hint of anything going on that shouldn't, and I—'

'They're hardly going to tell us.' Nathan rolled his eyes. 'It's our job to work that out.'

'Which is precisely why I asked them.' Jess wiped her mouth with a napkin. 'They should want to find out who murdered their boss.'

'You're barking up the wrong tree.'

'Maybe, maybe not,' Marsha butted in, unsure why her sergeant was so adamant everything was hunky-dory at the garage. 'Open mind, Nathan, and all that.'

Nathan scowled at her, and she raised her eyebrows until he looked away. Really?

'So who did you speak to that makes you so sure of yourself?'

Nathan shrugged. 'It was a feeling, that's all. You've known them all as long as me, longer, in fact.'

'Cheeky.'

'You can sense when people are lying. I didn't get that at all.'

'Maybe they don't know anything.' Connor tipped the remainder of his crisps down his throat. 'I mean, secrets are secrets, so how would they?'

'You mentioned Chris might be holding something back,' Jess said.

Nathan shook his head. 'She doesn't know these people like we do.'

'Don't speak about her as if she isn't here,' Marsha chided.

'But, boss, I—'

'Show some respect. Jess raised a valid point.'

'I've found nothing dodgy during my research so far,' Emma said, as if to ease the tension in the room. 'I'm working my way through a list that Jess got of employees and ex-employees. It goes back years.'

'Okay, thanks.' Marsha nodded. 'The business has been open since the eighties, so there might be hints of something to be found.'

Emma reached for a cake. 'I'm on it.'

'Well, as you know, I went to the mortuary for the formal identification of John Prophet and then we did the press conference. After that I spoke to his wife. Sylvia gave me details of the attack. She remembered what he looked like.'

Marsha went through the description given.

'She hasn't seen him before, and he turned up out of the blue. Unfortunately, she was out for the count after he swiped at her and didn't see what happened to John or the girls. She came round to find the man gone and then managed to raise the alarm.'

'So she thinks the girls are with him?' Jess queried.

'She didn't see what happened next. And that still doesn't tell us what our suspect's intentions were.' Marsha gnawed at her bottom lip. 'But, saving the best until last. Connor, do you want to tell them what you found out about the hit-and-run victim?'

'I do indeed.' Connor walked to the green noticeboard and pointed to an image, the one he'd retrieved from the Adams's household. 'Nicholas Adams, thirty-nine. Divorced with two children. Was living with his parents in Western Street until he found a place to stay after splitting with his wife. On further chatting to his parents, I found out that Nick was working as a mechanic at Prophet and Son.'

Jess's eyes widened, and she glanced at Nathan to see him doing the same.

'There were several people who didn't come in that morning,' Nathan confirmed. 'Apparently Dan told them to take as much time off as they needed. There were a lot of staff who'd worked there since leaving school. Some of them were really upset.'

Emma had her head down. 'Yes, he's on my list. I hadn't got to him yet.'

Connor updated them on his interview and then gave a theatrical bow.

'Wait a minute. I saw a photo in the reception area of the garage.' Jess got out her phone. 'There were five men on it. Two were John and Dan Prophet, and the third was the mechanic, Chris Osbourne.' She peered closer at the screen, pinching it to enlarge the image. 'I think the fourth one is Nicholas Adams. This is an old newspaper clipping. Perhaps there's a story online.'

Marsha held her hand out for the phone. 'Yes, that's him, all right. Do any of you know the fifth guy? He seems familiar to me, but I can't place him.'

The phone was passed around, but everyone drew a blank.

'Here it is,' Emma said. 'Prophet and Son were celebrating twenty years in business.'

They gathered around her computer screen while she read out the bulk of the article to them. 'Dan and Chris, nineteen back then, had been promoted to senior mechanics and the truck had been bought as they were expanding the business to do breakdown and recoveries.'

'Nathan, speak to Chris again. Try not to alarm him, but find out who the other man is.' Marsha glanced at the clock. 'I need to update Ryan.'

'Hold up before you do,' Emma cried just as she got to the door. 'I've found something else.'

CHAPTER TWENTY-NINE

'What have you got?' Marsha asked.

'An article in the *Leek News*,' Emma replied. 'It's dated a few months after the clip Jess saw in the reception at Prophet and Son. Shall I read some of it out?'

'Yes, go on.'

'The trial of Stephen Armstrong ended today with the nineteen-year-old receiving a sentence of three years for reckless driving. It followed the death of his sister, eight-year-old, Holly.'

'Oh, now I remember why I know him,' Marsha broke in. 'I was on the beat when that happened.'

'Armstrong,' Emma went on, 'was driving down Solomon's Hollow when he lost control of a blue Ford Fiesta. It came off the road, rolling several times before landing in a field. Holly was cut from the vehicle but was unconscious when taken by ambulance to the North Staffs Royal Infirmary.' She skim-read a bit more. 'Despite medical intervention, she never regained consciousness.'

'It was horrible,' Marsha said. 'I saw her body. It gave me nightmares for weeks.'

Marsha had been about to finish her shift when details of the crash came through. It was a lovely summer day, and she remembered wanting to rush home and get a few rays before the weekend was over.

She'd been in uniform then, and first on scene. The car had come off the road and was on its roof in the field next to it. With her colleague, PC Tim Ridley, they'd called it in, and then gone to see if they could help.

Stephen Armstrong had been out of the car, injured but walking wounded. He was distraught as he tried to wake his sister. It seemed Holly had taken the brunt of the crash after the car had hit a post before somersaulting.

Armstrong was arrested at the scene and taken to the station. The paperwork had taken hours, and it was dark when Marsha finally got home. It had been her who was inconsolable then.

'Shortly after the crash, Armstrong accused local business owner, John Prophet, of selling him an unsafe vehicle,' Emma went on. 'He claimed he had falsified the MOT certificate, the brakes had been faulty, and one of the front wheels had been loose. Despite thorough investigations by Staffordshire Police and the Traffic Collision Unit, the vehicle was deemed roadworthy. Witnesses behind Armstrong also saw him swerving, leaning back to talk to his sister who was in the back seat. Armstrong was breathalysed at the scene. The test was negative.'

'At least that's something,' Nathan noted.

'John Prophet, forty-eight, said he was pleased to have been cleared of any wrongdoing, despite always insisting everything said was untrue. "I'm glad Stephen has been brought to justice," he said. "My reputation could have been harmed but, even so, it doesn't bring Holly Armstrong back. That little girl lost her life at the hands of her brother, who should have been taking care of her. He deserves his time behind bars.'"

'When was that published?' Marsha wanted to know.

Emma scrolled up for the date. 'February, two thousand and four.'

'And remind me of the date when Holly died?'

'June thirtieth, two thousand and three.'

'That's twenty years ago this week,' Nathan noted. 'On Friday. Do we think Armstrong could be behind these attacks, perhaps for revenge?'

'Even though it was him who was in the wrong?' Connor frowned.

'Bring up his record,' Marsha told Emma.

Emma pulled it up and gasped at the list of convictions. 'He's been in and out of prison ever since. GBH, assault with intent, petty theft, even armed robbery.'

'Wasn't it enough that he lost his sister?' Marsha cried out in exasperation. 'He had to ruin his own life, too. Where is he living?'

'Bailed to a homeless unit a year ago. There's been nothing since.'

'We need to find him.' Marsha pointed to the board. 'Nathan, go and see Chris Osbourne, rather than ring. Explain the situation about the photo, but obviously don't mention anything else. We could have a situation on our hands, especially with two of them dead, and one of them has children missing. We also need to warn him to lay low for a while. Oh, and check why he wasn't in work on time on Monday morning.'

'On my way, boss.' He grabbed his car keys and was gone.

'If our killer is Stephen Armstrong,' Marsha continued, 'and he's getting revenge, why would he leave it so long?'

'He's been in and out of prison and not able to carry out his plan?' Connor queried.

'He's just come back to Leek after a long time away?' Jess suggested.

'It's because of the twenty-year anniversary of his sister's death, which he blamed the Prophets for?' Emma said.

'All food for thought,' Marsha agreed. 'If it is him, though. It could be anyone right now, including Chris Osbourne. So where are we going to find him? Is there a previous address?'

Emma checked the file on screen. 'Twenty-seven Hillcrest Avenue.'

'Okay. Connor, are you up for a recce? Talk to the neighbours if they're not there anymore. Emma, can you check Nicholas Adams's background and finances et cetera. His ex-wife, too, I think, before we need to ask her whereabouts at the time of the accident. Jess, you're with me. Let's go and talk to Dan and Lucy.'

CHAPTER THIRTY

'When can we go home?' Maisie asked Tamara. They were cuddled up together on the mattress.

'Soon,' Tamara replied. Even though it was warm in the room, she kept the blanket around them both.

Maisie had been crying for most of the night, sleeping sporadically and then wanting their mum when awakening. But the man kept banging on the door, shouting at her to be quiet, and she'd been frightened. Eventually, she'd cried herself to sleep.

During the night, flashbacks of what had happened to her gran and granddad flooded Tamara's mind. When the man had told them to run to him and not look, she had anyway. Her nan was asleep, but there was blood at the side of her head. Her granddad's eyes were wide open, and he was making strange wheezing noises.

All Tamara could concentrate on now was how she needed to keep her and Maisie safe until someone found them. People would be searching for them. Dad, Mum, the police. Everyone. They would find them and get them away from this man. All they had to do was behave until then. She had to try and keep Maisie quiet.

A door opened downstairs, and Maisie gasped.

'Is he coming?' she whispered, her bottom lip trembling as she reached for Tamara's hand.

They heard footsteps on the stairs, and they froze.

'I think so,' Tamara replied. 'Remember what I said? You need to do what he says, and don't make him angry.'

'Okay.'

The door was unlocked, and he stood there.

Tamara noticed he was wearing the same clothes as yesterday, his hair still greasy. He was carrying a tray with two plates and glasses of orange juice.

He stepped in the room and put it on the floor. 'I've made you something to eat.'

Tamara stayed where she was until he left the room.

As soon as the lock was turned, she pulled back the blanket and fetched the tray. She left the drinks on it, passing a plate to Maisie, and then got back into bed.

'This is nice,' she said, taking a small bite of the sandwich and trying her best to swallow it. She wasn't hungry, but she had to keep her strength up.

'I don't like this ham,' Maisie said.

'I think you'd better eat it. Mum will be pleased when I tell her.'

Maisie seemed satisfied by this.

Tamara didn't want to think about being there for lunch tomorrow. She wanted to go home, just as much as Maisie.

He took his chance and left the house through the back door, moving quietly so that the girls wouldn't know he'd gone out. His visit wouldn't take long, and he could be back within half an hour.

Every afternoon around two o'clock, he'd been visiting his father in the Blue Meadow Hospice. He wasn't sure why, as Edwin was mostly asleep when he got there.

Edwin was getting weaker by the day. The doctors had said it wouldn't be long now, and at least they were keeping him as comfortable as they could.

The door to his father's room was closed, so he knocked quietly and went in.

Edwin was tucked up in bed, a wisp of himself after his illness, the machines around his bed monitoring his rapid deterioration.

How he'd hated what had happened to them all through the years. Edwin Armstrong had let the accident, his sister's death, take over his dark thoughts even more than he had.

It was all their fault, the Prophet family.

'Hello, son, I didn't think you'd be here today.'

'Thought I'd pop by. How are you doing?'

'So-so.' Edwin coughed, as if he'd smoked twenty cigarettes a day all his life, and yet he hadn't touched one in decades. The damage was done before he'd quit, though. Lung cancer. He knew he was dying.

He handed his dad a glass of water, held it while he sipped a little from a straw. Despite their love-hate relationship, it was hard seeing him getting weaker by the day.

He drew up a chair and sat down by the side of the bed.

'Thanks, lad,' Edwin mumbled.

That was all the conversation he got from him. It was less than a minute before Edwin was asleep.

Outside, the sound of voices and laughter filtered in, bursting into the silence. He tried to think of the last time he'd shared a proper conversation with someone. The last time *he'd* laughed like that. His life was so meaningless.

A few minutes later, there was a knock at the door, and a woman stepped inside. He'd seen her before, almost every day since his dad has been transferred from hospital to the hospice. She was in her mid-thirties, auburn hair tied back from her face, her fringe dropping into her eyes. The purple uniform of tunic and trousers looked a bit tight.

'Only me, Edwin. Come to – Oh, hello. I thought you'd be gone by now. I can come back later.'

'No, it's fine,' he said. 'I was just leaving anyway. I see there's no change.'

'No, but he's comfortable. I'm Janine, if you need me for anything anytime.' The woman rested a hand on his shoulder.

He found he wanted her to leave it there. He hadn't had physical contact with a female in a good many years, and it felt nice.

He stayed for a few more minutes and then left her to it. He didn't want to leave those girls for too long. It was bad enough trying to keep them quiet at night, never mind during the day, and he had a few more things to do before he decided what to do with them.

CHAPTER THIRTY-ONE

'This is going to be a tough call,' Marsha told Jess as they parked outside the Prophets' home. 'But hopefully Dan can shed some light on things.'

PC Joy opened the door.

'How's everything?' Marsha asked, her voice low. She'd rung ahead to say that she and Jess were on their way.

'Calm at the moment,' Rachel said. 'But I think they'd been expecting news when you called.'

Marsha closed her eyes momentarily. Of course they would jump to conclusions. They wanted their family together again.

'What about you? Any problems?'

'No, I'm fine, thanks. I've had to shoo away the press twice, but nothing I can't handle.'

'Idiots,' Marsha growled. 'Have they no compassion?'

With nothing further to report, they were shown into the living room, a large and airy space with cream furnishings and checked floor-length curtains either side of a picture window that almost spanned the whole back wall.

Dan stood up, and Lucy moved to the edge of the settee on spotting them.

'Is there any news about our girls?' Dan wanted to know.

'It's been two days, and I can't bear another night not knowing where they are,' Lucy said.

'I'm sorry, no,' Marsha replied. 'We have so many officers out looking for them, and the appeal that you did with me earlier is bringing in lots of calls from the public. We're dealing with them now. We're also doing regular updates on social media.'

'Has *anyone* seen them?' Lucy shook her head, tears welling in her eyes. 'The waiting is unbearable. I keep wondering what they're going through.'

'Don't.' Dan moved to sit with her.

'How's Sylvia today?' Marsha asked, hoping to get on to something slightly better.

'She's bearing up, thanks. She'll be moving in with us for a while when she gets out of hospital. There's a lot to sort out, but she says she wants to stay at the farm. Time will tell, I guess.' Dan shook his head. 'If I was her, I wouldn't want to set foot in there ever again.'

'I can understand that. Lucy, Dan.' Marsha sat down, Jess following suit. 'We need to ask you a few more questions as certain things have come to light.'

Lucy glanced fleetingly at Dan and, for a moment, Marsha saw a sign of something. Was it nerves? Guilt? Hard to tell, but it definitely needed probing.

'My colleague went to visit The Station this morning. He saw footage of you and your dad arguing, Dan. Can you tell us what about?'

'I never saw that.' Lucy frowned. 'When was this?'

'It was when I went to the toilet,' Dan explained. 'Dad was waiting for me outside. He wanted to know about the business, poking his nose in, telling me how to keep on top of things. I told him I had it all under control, but he wouldn't let it rest. I don't think he ever wanted to retire, so he found it hard at times to step away.'

Marsha saw Jess making a few notes. Dan had made a fair enough comment, she supposed, after what they'd learned.

'I also sent my officers to chat to the staff at Prophet and Son, as you know.' Jess passed Marsha a photocopy of the image from the wall, and she handed it to Dan before continuing. 'While they were there, one of them spotted a photo in the reception area, with five men on it.'

Dan looked at it. 'It was taken when my dad had been in business for twenty years. Dad hated it as Stephen Armstrong was on it, but he wouldn't get rid of it because it was an important day for the business.'

Marsha nodded. 'We know that you and your dad are on there, and Chris Osbourne. I'm not sure if you've heard about the hit-and-run last night? The victim has been identified as Nicholas Adams, who died of his injuries. We're treating that as murder, too.'

'Not Nick as well?' Lucy cried out as if in pain.

'Oh, no.' Dan gripped onto the arm of the settee, his fingers turning white at the knuckles. 'His poor parents. I must go and see them.'

'We're sorry for your loss. As you can imagine, we needed to locate the fifth person in the photo, so one of my officers spoke to Chris Osbourne, who also confirmed that it was Stephen.'

'His father, Edwin, worked at the garage, too, until the accident. Edwin left not long after the photo was taken.' He frowned as things started to sink in. 'Are you saying Steve is involved somehow?'

'Everything is circumstantial at the moment. But we do need to locate him to eliminate him from our enquiries. We've warned Chris to stay vigilant, and if he's in any danger, we'll suggest taking him into custody for his own safety. But we also need to make certain that someone isn't out to get at you, too, Dan.'

'Me?' Dan frowned. 'Why would anyone want to come after me?'

'Is that why our girls are missing?' Lucy asked.

'We can't be certain of that,' Marsha cautioned.

'But you don't know! Has someone taken them to get back at the family?' Lucy glared at Dan. 'Well? Do you know?'

'Of course I bloody don't!'

'Dan, is there anything you can tell us about Stephen?' Marsha asked next. She hoped that if she ignored their outburst, their frustration would fizzle out. 'Or Edwin?'

'No. I haven't seen either of them in years.'

'Since Holly was killed?'

'Yes.'

'Is that the girl who died at Solomon's Hollow?' Lucy seemed perplexed. 'What does she have to do with this?'

Marsha quickly went through the details of the accident that happened twenty years ago. 'Can you remember anything we should know about what happened at the time, Dan?'

'Such as?'

'Any fall outs? Things that didn't add up?'

'There was some sort of bust up between my dad and Edwin. When Stephen was charged with dangerous driving, after Holly's death, Edwin had a go at Dad. He told him to leave, but it got out of hand and a fight broke out. That's all I can remember.'

'Why didn't you tell us this before?'

'I hadn't even thought about it until you mentioned Edwin's name.' He sat forward. '*Is* this to do with Steve? Is he the one behind all this? Does he have our girls?'

'We're following all leads at the moment, Dan,' Marsha soothed. 'We will let you know as soon as we find anything out. There's just one more thing. How well do you know Chris Osbourne?'

'We've known each other since we were in junior school. He's a really good mate. Why?'

'He's on the photo, too, and—'

'Chris won't have anything to do with this.' Dan shook his head.

'We have to look into every possibility. That's why we need to confirm Chris's whereabouts yesterday morning. I believe he was late arriving at the garage. Would you happen to know why?'

Marsha kept her gaze on Lucy's. She was blushing furiously.

'I don't know. Maybe he had a medical or something. I'd have to check with him.' Dan turned to face Lucy. 'You don't know why, do you?'

His words were emphasised so much that Marsha and Jess automatically glanced at each other.

'No.' Lucy's voice came out as a squeak, and she cleared her throat. 'He never mentioned it to me. I haven't seen him since last week, though.'

Finally, Marsha and Jess said their goodbyes, quietly urging Rachel to get in touch if necessary.

Walking back to the car, Jess spoke first. 'Is Lucy seeing Chris Osbourne on the side, boss?'

'That was your impression, too?' Marsha asked. 'He told Nathan he forgot to set his alarm. That's the lamest excuse ever, but hard to disprove, although he doesn't have anyone to corroborate it for him either way. I think another visit to the garage is in order tomorrow morning. See what he has to say for himself.

'As well, why hasn't Dan mentioned what Sarah Cradford told you? Is it because Lucy doesn't know that the business still solely belongs to his father?'

CHAPTER THIRTY-TWO

Nathan hadn't been expecting to finish early enough to see daylight. But after they'd checked out everything they could, Marsha had sent the team home.

There was no lead on Stephen Armstrong yet. His parents had moved out of Hillcrest Avenue, a rented property, and the new owners didn't know where they'd gone to. Connor had left a contact card in case they heard anything, but for now, the lead was a dead end.

It was just after nine p.m., and the town of Leek was alive. Nathan loved and hated the warmer months in equal measures.

As a person, he enjoyed nothing more than sitting out with friends, having a laugh over a beer or two.

As a police officer, he knew that the inevitable fights and neighbour disputes amplified with the longer daylight hours, time spent outdoors and warmer weather. Sometimes people went too far, and it would often leave a family grieving a loved one.

He'd decided to grab a quick shower at home and then head down to his local pub to see who was about. A couple of pints would be good for the soul.

But once he was ready, he found himself thinking of his wife, Amy, and wondering if she would let him see Daisy that weekend. The weather was set to hold for a few more days. If he wasn't working, maybe Daisy could stay over, and he'd set up a barbecue, just the two of them.

Without a further thought, he hopped in his car and drove to his old address.

It still upset him how alien it now felt as he walked up the path, especially when he had to ring the doorbell.

A few seconds later, he saw a shadow appear behind the glass and the door opened.

Amy was tanned, looking well. She was wearing a sleeveless dress, showing off toned arms and long legs. Bare feet with vibrant pink painted toenails and blonde hair in a sexy up-do had his stomach lurching.

It hit him right in the gut that she was moving on and he wasn't.

He wanted a second chance but knew she'd never give him one. He didn't deserve it either.

Amy folded her arms. 'I thought I told you to ring before calling round.'

'I've been leaving you messages for the past three days and you've been ignoring them, so you gave me no choice.' He cursed inwardly. The blame game wasn't how he'd intended starting the conversation. 'I'd like to see Daisy this weekend. I haven't seen her in—'

'She won't be here. We're going away on Friday evening, until Sunday afternoon. To the Lakes.'

He swallowed, another punch landing fully in the stomach. 'We, as in you and Daisy?'

'Yes, I mean me and Daisy.'

'She'll tell me if someone else goes with you.'

'Not that it has anything to do with you if they were. You gave up that right three months ago.'

Nathan cringed. It seemed he hadn't been away long enough yet to be forgiven. Instead, they resorted to arguing on the doorstep.

His silence as he gazed at the ground must have got to her because he heard her sigh. When he glanced up again, she'd dropped her arms.

'Okay, okay. You can have her this weekend. She misses you, you know. Counts down the days until she sees you again.'

His heart filled with love for the little girl he wanted back in his life on a daily basis. 'Really?'

'Really.' She glanced at her watch. 'You can come up and see her for a minute, if you try not to wake her.'

Nathan nodded, unable to believe his luck. He hadn't been inside the house for two months, not since he'd stopped pleading with her to have him back.

He tiptoed up the stairs. The door to Daisy's room was ajar, and he popped his head around it first. Daisy was flat out, her arms either side of her face, one foot peeping out from underneath the duvet. Her hair was messed up already, wisps sticking to her forehead due to the heat.

Nathan hadn't thought it was possible to love anyone so much until he'd had Daisy. He thought he loved Amy, but it was a different kind of love. Everyone said it to you when you were going to be a dad, and it was hard to comprehend until it happened.

He walked over slowly, desperate for Daisy to wake up and see her old man had come to see her, but equally knowing he should let her sleep. He kneeled down beside her, his ankle cracking loudly.

Daisy's eyes opened, and she turned to him.

'Daddy?' she whispered. 'What are you doing here?'

'Thought I'd come to say hello.'

''Lo.' Daisy's eyes closed again.

It wasn't fair to keep her awake, even though Nathan wanted a conversation and a hug before leaving, so he stood up to leave.

Amy was in the doorway, making him jump.

'She's just like her dad. Falls asleep in seconds,' she whispered. 'But at least she doesn't snore.'

They shared a smile. Nathan knew the wonderful moment wouldn't last, and he'd do anything to turn back the clock, so instead he made arrangements to collect Daisy on Friday evening from school, work permitting, and left.

For once, it had been a good end to the day, and he still had time to join his mates in the local for a pint or two. Maybe taking his mind off everything would do him good.

CHAPTER THIRTY-THREE

Marsha had been to see Ryan to give him another update. Afterwards, she'd finished what paperwork she needed to do in preparation for the next day. But she couldn't get the Prophet girls from her mind.

Ryan had asked her to join him tomorrow morning, hoping to get Dan and Lucy to attend the press conference to speak to the camera again, if nothing came in overnight. He wanted to keep things fresh in the public eye. Someone knew where those girls were.

It was their second night away. Marsha felt as if she should be doing more to find them, but, equally, knew she and her team were doing all they could, along with the wider force.

They were utilising the public, and since the appeal that morning, social media was abuzz again with photos of the missing girls. Ryan reassured her that, with all their work in the background, he trusted her to get what they needed.

He'd also told her to go home and get some rest.

She sat back in her chair. Although Connor, Nathan, and Emma had gone about half an hour ago, Jess still had her head down. They'd been looking further into Stephen Armstrong's whereabouts, but they'd found nothing. He wasn't on the electoral roll, which could mean a number of things. Either he moved around, sofa surfed, or had never bothered to register himself.

It was half past nine. There was nothing else they could do for now. She came out of her office and stood in the doorway.

'Fancy a drink before we leave for the night? It'd be nice, just you and me, and honestly, I'm not in the mood to go home straight away.'

Jess threw her arms in the air and stretched out her back. 'Yeah, why not.'

They switched off their computers and headed out of the building, dodging the officers who were swapping shifts.

'Hey, Jeff, how's that son of yours doing?' Marsha shouted out to a man at the far end of the corridor.

'Oh, he's doing great, thanks, Marsha.' Jeff beamed. 'He'll be home soon, but not for long, I imagine.'

'Jeff's youngest, Freddie. He's been in the US for a few months.' She glanced at Jess who was smirking. 'What? A small town like this, and you get to know everyone. Much better than being in a big place, I think.'

'I'll defer on answering that until I've been here a while.'

They smiled at each other.

'What's your poison?' Marsha asked as they exited the building into the last hour of the evening.

'If I wasn't driving it would be a G and T or a red wine. As it is, I'll have a lemonade.'

'I could down a double vodka, but I guess I'll go for just the one. Mind, I can leave my car here and pick it up in the morning. I only live a ten-minute walk away. You should stay over one night, and we could go out for a meal.'

'That would be great, thanks. Anything to get away from

my mum. I love her, but she's a fusspot. She treats me like I'm ten years old. Are your parents still around?'

'Mum is. Dad died sixteen years ago, when I was twenty-three, just after I joined the force.'

It was still early enough for there to be lots of people milling about outside. Groups of friends standing on the pavements. Couples loved-up, eyeing each other across the tables. Marsha smiled as she spotted a few girls in strappy sandals and summer dresses, all giggles and chatter. Ah, to be young again.

'When we went for a night out, wearing heels on these cobbles would have been a nightmare,' Jess remarked. 'I'm so glad fashion has changed over the years and that it's more acceptable to wear flats now.'

'Me, too,' Marsha agreed. 'My preference in summer is Converse, and winter it's Docs. I bet you were spoiled for choice with all the shops in Manchester.'

'That's probably the only thing I will miss.'

'Not planning on going back again, you know, when you're ready for sergeant?'

'Not at all.'

'That sounds adamant.'

Jess went quiet.

Outside The Old Jug, Marsha spotted a vacant table and pointed to it. 'Grab that, and I'll get the drinks in.'

The bar was two deep, so while she waited to be served, Marsha glanced around. The pub was one of her favourite places, most of the officers at the station, too. She waved when she spotted a few more off-duty cops over in the far corner. She could see they were grateful for a pint at the end of the evening.

Out of the window, her attention fell on Jess. Either she was people watching or miles away, deep in thought. She didn't even spot Marsha coming back until she put the glasses in front of her.

'Are you okay?' she asked. 'We don't know each other that well yet, but I sense something is bothering you. Want to talk about it?'

'I'm not sure it will do any use.'

Marsha moved seats so that she was next to Jess rather than across from her.

'Okay, let me go first then. I've been married for nineteen years. I have two wonderful daughters, but I think me and Phil are over. Honestly, I get more attention from my dog, Larry.' She sighed. 'I think he's having an affair. Phil, not Larry.'

Jess gave a faint smile. 'I'm so sorry.' She turned towards her slightly.

It was the first time Marsha had aired her thoughts. Things had obviously been more strained between them than she'd realised.

'I haven't said anything because, well, I don't have anyone to tell. I'm certainly not sharing it with my team. But sometimes, you have to spill.'

'Does Phil know about your suspicions?'

'I'm not sure, but he wants to talk.'

'Oh.' Jess nodded her head knowingly.

'Thing is, I'm frightened to, because even though I'm not sure I want to be with him anymore, I don't want to do anything about it. Finishing it seems way scarier.'

'You can't go through the rest of your life unhappy, just because you're scared.'

'That's what I've been mulling over for the past few months. Am I willing to put up with it, or would I be better off alone?'

'Only you will have the answer to that. How old are your girls?'

'Suzanne is eighteen, and Cassie sixteen. One is finishing A levels, and the other GCSEs. I think they realise things aren't going well. We rarely spend time as a family. The girls aren't in a lot now, so it's even more obvious to them when they are that something isn't right. On Sunday, Cassie asked me if we were going to get divorced. I don't think they'll see it as a problem, given their ages. I expect they want us to be happy. It would be different if they were younger, I guess.'

'How do you keep all that to yourself?' Jess shook her head.

'Like I said, I had no one to tell, until now.' Marsha took another sip of her drink. 'Your turn. What's bothering you?'

CHAPTER THIRTY-FOUR

Marsha glanced over the square where a group of teenagers were noisily walking past, pushing and shoving each other in jest.

'My DI. We used to be an item,' Jess said eventually.

'Ah. So it's over for good?'

'Too bloody right, it is.'

Marsha was taken aback by her tone. It was the first time she'd seen Jess angry. She wondered what had made her that way.

'We were together for two years. At first, he was lovely. He was on a different syndicate, so we didn't see each other a lot at work.'

'Oh, yes, you big shots in Manchester have several major crime teams, whereas in the outback, we have just the one.'

'You only need the one, luckily!' Jess exclaimed. 'Anyway, I moved in with him after a few months, and then he changed. You know, you read the stories all the time about it and yet you never think it will happen to you. It wasn't until it was almost too late that I realised I needed to get away from him.'

'What happened?'

'He attacked me one night. I'd been on a double shift, halfway through a murder inquiry where some lad had been stabbed by his best mate. Apparently, he'd seen me that day, talking to one of my colleagues, and accused me of flirting with him, sleeping with him actually. There was nothing going on, but he wouldn't let it go. It was as if he wanted a reason to hate me.'

'The bastard.'

'Looking back, I can't believe I stayed with him for so long. But, like you, it seemed easier. Before that it was all insults and coercive control. But when he slapped me one night, I sensed that would be the first of many if I didn't leave.'

'Double bastard!'

The rowdy group went inside the pub, and it was quieter again.

'I stayed with a friend until I got my own flat, which didn't go down well even though she was female. He found out where it was, followed me home one night and tried to get in. I can handle my own for the most part, but he wouldn't take no for an answer. That's when the stalking began. Text messages, phone calls until I changed my number. Notes left on my car windscreen. I couldn't do anything without seeing him somewhere in the background.'

'Did you mention this to anyone? At work, I mean?'

Jess shook her head. 'Stupidly, I thought he'd give up after a while. But then he was transferred to my syndicate. He made my life hell on a daily basis, giving me all the menial tasks, making me stop behind and do extra work, showing me up in front of everyone, that kind of thing. In the end, he was pulled in by the DCI and told to back off. That's when I put in for a transfer.'

'I still can't believe this sort of thing goes on,' Marsha

sympathised. 'You should be able to report him and get something done, not have the problems brushed under the carpet.'

'I know, but I felt it would make things worse.'

'That's just it, you shouldn't feel that way. I've a good mind to complain for you.'

'No, please don't.' Jess welled up without warning.

'I wouldn't.' Marsha touched her arm. 'I just meant I hate to hear about someone being treated like that.'

'He sent me flowers yesterday, wishing me luck on my first shift. Said he was missing me. I had to keep them because my mum would get suspicious if I dumped them in the bin. Which is what I wanted to do.'

'Do you think he'll come here and hound you once you're settled?'

'I'm hoping he'll give up eventually, but yes, I think there will be some pestering. He doesn't like to lose.'

'Then I suggest we get our boxing gloves ready, because he's not getting past us without a fight.'

Jess smiled, clinking her glass with Marsha's. 'I like the sound of that.'

Marsha got home to an empty house. The family noticeboard showed Cassie was studying with April, and Suzanne was working so she wouldn't be back until around midnight. She wondered where Phil was, perhaps still at work. It meant she could relax, but equally she didn't want to be alone.

Too tired to make anything to eat, she sliced off a huge chunk of cheese and sat down with a glass of red wine.

Usually when the house was quiet, she would relish the silence. But, with Phil wanting to talk, and sensing things were coming to a head, she wondered if she'd even be sitting here in a few months.

Although most of the mortgage was paid, she couldn't

afford the house on one salary. They had two years of payments before it would be theirs. But it was too much for her to cope with alone. The heating costs were astronomical.

Marsha remembered the day she and Phil had moved in. The property had been a total wreck, taking them seven years to renovate.

It had been a steal of a price because of that, but it had also become a money pit. The whole place needed rewiring, and new plumbing, throughout. Wooden floors had to be ripped up and replaced. The kitchen and dining room were knocked into one large airy space, bathrooms refitted.

Eventually, they'd got it how they wanted. She and Phil made the smaller bedroom on the first floor into a den where they could be alone if Suzanne and Cassie had friends round.

The top floor had been rigged out for the girls. They each had a large bedroom, and as the third had led into the bathroom, it had first become a playroom and then a dressing room.

Marsha loved that they had their own space and told them often how lucky they were. As a child, she'd had to share with her brother in a two-up, two-down terraced house, and when he'd died, it hadn't ever felt like home again.

But this place had always been the heart of their family. Marsha wouldn't leave unless she had to. She couldn't. She was so proud of it. It would break her to sell it.

There were so many memories among its walls.

Bringing first Suzanne, and then Cassie, home from the hospital.

Having one drink too many on Christmas Eve, sneaking down the stairs with gifts from Santa and Phil falling and hurting his back, unable to sit at the table for dinner the next day.

Suzanne splitting her head open after braking too hard on her bike and going over the handlebars.

Cassie's face when she'd first set eyes on Larry as a pup.

Playing games around the kitchen table, then in later years, it had all been about dancing around the floor listening to Sophie Ellis-Bextor during lockdowns when Coronavirus was at its peak.

Now, she felt blessed that her girls were at the age where they were good company.

Marsha didn't want any of that to change, despite both her daughters getting old enough to take their next steps into adulthood. At least the recent cost-of-living rises might mean they had to stay at home for longer now. Yet, she could still remember when they were as young as Tamara and Maisie Prophet.

She sat for half an hour until her silence was interrupted. Cassie was home, and Larry was barking his welcome. She went through to the kitchen to make coffee.

Perhaps Cassie would help her mum to unwind and forget the umpteen things she had running through her mind.

CHAPTER THIRTY-FIVE

Wednesday

Marsha drove along Buxton Road, Larry panting in the back of the vehicle behind the dog guard. It was early again, overcast but warm, promises of another nice day ahead.

At least she hadn't had to speak to Phil yet. She'd gone to bed before he'd come in and sneaked out of it before he awoke.

As she drove towards Solomon Hollow before the ascent up to The Roaches, she noticed a flash of colour. It was a bunch of flowers, wrapped in pink cellophane.

She'd only had a quick glimpse, but it didn't seem as though it had been there long: she couldn't recall seeing them on Sunday morning.

There wasn't anywhere to turn around, so she'd look more closely on her return journey.

So much had happened in three short days since her last trip there. Two men murdered, possibly by the same suspect, and others warned in case they were future victims. Emma was continuing to check through CCTV for sightings of the white van, hoping to link it to the hit-and-run, but there was nothing yet.

It was beginning to make sense that Armstrong could be their killer, although they were a long way from having the evidence to prove it. The question was, where was he now? Still in Leek, or further afield?

They needed to find him, to eliminate him from their enquiries at least. She'd have to see if Ryan was willing to give out his name to the public yet. Then Scarlett Hilton could get the press more involved in flushing him out.

Having said that, there was no clear evidence, so Ryan might not buy that angle. Letting people know about someone was usually a last resort in case they got it wrong.

She parked up, clipped on Larry's lead, and let him out of the vehicle. 'Come on, fella. Let's walk off the cobwebs.'

When they were away from the road and she could see no one around, she let him loose. He was a good dog with recall, always coming back when called, but if she saw anyone, Marsha would pop the lead back on. For now, Larry could stretch his legs.

After forty minutes, her head was much clearer. She felt more positive about the day ahead and eager for breakfast. But first she needed to stop at Solomon's Hollow.

Driving towards it, she thought how steep the dip was, and how it was easy to lose control. Her foot hovered over the brake at all times, until she was ready to rev up the other side.

She approached the spot and pulled in on the grass verge as far as possible, popping on her hazard lights. Traffic was getting busier, but there was nowhere to park.

'Won't be a minute,' she told Larry.

She jogged across to the flowers. Once there, she noticed there was an old photograph tucked inside the cellophane.

She went back to the car for a pair of gloves. Slipping them on, she took out the image for further inspection.

It was of a young girl and a teenage boy, dressed in summer clothes. Holly and Stephen, she assumed, the similarities between them and the newspaper article she'd seen speaking volumes. They were both smiling, the girl sitting on a swing and the boy behind her waiting to push it.

They seemed to be in a rear garden. Fencing from the next-door house was visible at the side of a lawn, and there were houses in the background.

Marsha turned it over, but there was nothing written on the back. Shame.

She glanced around, again remembering the heartbreaking feelings of being there when the accident had happened.

Could it have been Stephen who had visited?

She wanted to take the items with her, yet at the same time felt disrespectful moving them. They might retrieve fingerprints, but they'd probably need a warrant to remove anything. For now, she took some photos to show her team. She could always send someone to retrieve them if necessary.

An hour later, she arrived at the station, relieved to see Jess in and looking perkier that morning. She smiled at her.

'It was good to get together last night. I enjoyed our chat. Thanks for listening.'

'Works both ways.' Jess grinned. 'It did me good to tell someone, to be honest.'

'Me, too. Bloody men.'

They laughed, sharing their first in-joke.

The rest of the team arrived in the next fifteen minutes and, once drinks were made, they sat together discussing the previous day's events, as well as Marsha's trip out that morning.

'While I feel helpless that there have been no sightings of Tamara and Maisie Prophet for forty-eight hours, at least we know how many officers are still searching for them. Our main task now is to find Stephen Armstrong,' Marsha added. 'I expect Ryan will be in to give me a bollocking soon as we have no concrete leads, except a ghost we can't locate yet.'

'Boss, I've been sent some new footage of a white van that went tearing along the road just before the hit-and-run happened,' Connor said. 'It's small and knackered, like the one we might be after.'

Marsha went to stand behind him as he showed her on the screen. There wasn't much to see, to be fair, but it could lead to more. 'It might be the same van that was parked at the top of Berry Lane Farm. Does it show a number plate?'

'Only a bit of one so far.'

'Pass it to Emma, and I'll get her to check with DVLA. Worth seeing if it was spotted anywhere else afterwards, too.'

'On it, boss.'

Marsha went into her office, closing the door for the first time in ages. Then she picked up her phone and rang a colleague of hers, Martin Bailey, who had transferred to GMP and was a DI now, too. He was also someone who could be trusted not to share details of the call.

'Marsha! Good to hear from you. What are you after?'

'Do I have to want something to call you?' She laughed.

'Well, no, but it's usually the case. So?'

'Okay, it's a little bit delicate, but what can you tell me about Reece Masters?'

CHAPTER THIRTY-SIX

Lucy was nervous. Dan had barely said a word to her since the police had left the night before. She'd gone to bed on her own, and he hadn't come upstairs to her knowledge.

At eight o'clock that morning, Rachel was up and on duty. Dan had still stayed out of their way. Now, an hour later, he was sitting in the kitchen, eyes on the garden, mind clearly elsewhere.

She went upstairs, unsure what to do with herself. It was then he came into the bedroom to her.

'Do you know where Chris was on Monday morning?' he asked, standing in the doorway.

Lucy closed her eyes momentarily, unable to look at him.

'Was he here?' He marched over to her.

'I...'

'Well, was he?'

Lucy couldn't deny it any longer. She nodded.

'Why?' he seethed. 'Of course, I know, but I want to hear it from you.'

'Dan, I—' Lucy reached for his arm, but he shrugged her hand away.

'Don't touch me,' he seethed. 'You were with him, here at our house? While our girls were in danger, and my parents were attacked? My father is dead!'

'I didn't know that was going to happen!'

'So that's okay, is it?' He sniggered. 'At least Chris has an alibi now. He couldn't have murdered my father.'

'He would never do that!'

'No? You think you know him, but you have no idea. For the past few months, he's been pressuring me into going into partnership with him! All the bloody time. He said it was his right, after working at the garage for so long. Maybe that was why he wanted to get *close* to you. So he could sweet talk you into helping him get his own way.'

'No.' Lucy shook her head, but already she was doubting herself. 'That can't be true.'

'How would you know? I thought I knew you well until this morning.' His hands went to his hair, and he pulled at it. 'Why would you do that to me? Don't you have everything you need right here?'

'No, actually, I don't!' Even though she was in the wrong, Lucy felt the need to defend her position. 'You're always at work, and I was lonely.'

'Please, spare me the excuses. You can't blame anyone but yourself for this. And Chris, I've known him for more than thirty years. Some mate he turned out to be, the fucking leech,' Dan grabbed his car keys.

'Where are you going?'

'For a drive, I can't stand to be in the same room as you.'

'Wait, Dan,' Lucy cried. "Please, don't go. We can sort this out.'

'Like hell we can.' He left the house with the slam of the front door.

Lucy burst into tears. What a mess. She was empty inside, unsure how she felt now that Dan knew about her affair.

Monday morning had been all about seeing Chris, but the hurt on Dan's face had wounded her. It made her realise how much she cared for him.

How could she have done that to him?

And how awful for him to find out now, of all times. He must think he married a right bitch.

Actually, he had. Because she'd had a choice. When she and Chris had started flirting, she could have stopped it there. But she was the one who had instigated their first meeting.

She'd been upset after having an argument with Dan, about him working so late every evening. So when Chris had asked her what was wrong, she'd confided in him. He'd comforted her by saying he'd love to be with someone like her, and that Dan didn't deserve her. She'd kissed him then, like a fool.

Was Dan right about Chris? Had he only been trying to get her sweet, so she could persuade Dan to go into business with him? Because it hadn't seemed like that at the time.

Why did this have to happen now? Lucy had far too much to think about with her girls missing. Her life was meaningless until they were found, regardless of anything else. But even so, she had to warn Chris. She reached for her phone and left him a message.

If the police come to ask where you were on Monday morning, you can tell them that you were with me. Dan knows. He knows everything, and he's so mad.

CHAPTER THIRTY-SEVEN

Nathan saw Chris Osbourne's face drop when he walked into the garage. He pointed to the office.

'Could I have another word?'

Chris followed him inside and closed the door behind them. Outside, some of the staff had already gathered in a group. He saw them glancing over.

'As you know, Chris, we're trying to locate Stephen Armstrong at the moment. What can you remember about a fight between John Prophet and Edwin Armstrong, before Edwin was sacked?'

Nathan could see he seemed relieved, but he was saving the harder questions until later.

'That's going back a bit. If I recall correctly, Edwin was mad as hell about his daughter's death. He accused John of faking the MOT to get a sale. Which was ridiculous. We all knew if anyone, Edwin would have pulled a fast one.'

'What do you mean?'

'He was a crap mechanic, always doing the minimum, and sometimes not even that. Why do you ask?'

'Just checking things out.' Nathan hoped Chris wouldn't

lie to him. All he wanted was to confirm his alibi. 'Now, onto more personal matters. Where were you on Monday morning, between the hours of eight and nine?'

Chris didn't have time to reply before the door was flung open and Dan stormed into the room.

'What the fuck have you been doing with my wife?' He lunged at Chris, catching him on the chin with a balled fist. 'You two-faced bastard.'

Chris pushed back his chair to avoid being hit again.

'Dan!' Nathan held him back. 'Calm down.'

'Screwing Lucy when my dad was dying?' Dan went on, spittle flying across the room. 'What was it, pillow talk, so that she'd put in a good word for you? Ever since Dad retired, you've been after me to partner up with you. Was that why you did it?'

'No!' Chris shook his head, his hands up in a plea. 'And I didn't know that was going to happen to John.'

'I want you out of here. You're fired, do you hear me? Don't even think about taking me to court for wrongful dismissal. If you do, I'll make sure you're ruined in this town.' He tried to get at Chris again.

'That's enough, Dan!' Nathan cried.

Dan flopped down in a chair, anger deflating in an instant, and buried his head in his hands.

'Go home,' Nathan said to him.

'To what? I don't have anything left.'

'Of course you do. You just can't see that at the moment.' Nathan opened the door and shouted to one of the staff, 'Dan needs a coffee. Sort him out, will you?'

Alone again with Chris, he continued his questioning. 'Why don't you run me through the right version of events on Monday morning?'

'I was with Lucy, at her house. We'd arranged to meet

because we knew Dan was going to Buxton and the girls were with their grandparents.'

'What time did you arrive?'

'Just after eight. I stayed for about an hour and then I came to work. The cameras will back me up.'

Nathan would certainly be getting someone to check into that. 'Why didn't you tell us at the time?'

'John Prophet said that I would be made a partner with Dan when he finished. But when push came to shove, after his retirement party he told me he'd changed his mind. I gave my life to this firm thinking I would get my reward. Me and Dan worked well together.'

Nathan couldn't help his eyebrows rising in surprise.

'I know I messed up, but I love Dan like a brother, and I hated what I was doing. However, if I'd known John was lying, I wouldn't have stuck around for half my working life. It stings, big time, that he would do that to me. We had an argument last week about it, and I thought if I mentioned it, you might think it was me who'd killed him.'

'I can understand that part at least. Right now, I need you to stay vigilant until we find out who has committed these crimes.' Nathan deemed it only fair to let him know their thoughts around the photograph, the hit-and-run, and stress again why he might be in danger. 'For now, keep a low profile if you can.'

Chris sniggered. 'Oh, I think there's every possibility of that. I doubt I'll have anyone left on my side once this gets out.'

Nathan gave him his contact details. 'Don't hesitate to call if you're worried about anything.'

Back in the car, he made a quick call to Rachel to ask her to check in with Lucy to see if what Chris was saying tallied with her version of events. If so, Chris was off the hook.

So, did that only leave Stephen Armstrong?

CHAPTER THIRTY-EIGHT

Tamara woke up, startled by a noise. She listened, lying still and quiet, but there was nothing.

She started to cry again, quietly so as not to wake Maisie, even though her eyes were still sore from the night before.

Having Maisie with her had been comforting, but she wanted to go home, too. Being in this room was horrible, and she was so scared.

She tried to hide it, so that Maisie wouldn't get too upset, but all she could think about was what would happen to them. They'd been in this room for two nights, and this was their third day. The room was smelly, and she wanted to get out of it. But there was nothing she could do.

Instead, she thought about the things she missed. Her mum and dad. Her friends, her gran and granddad. Her rabbit, Tiny, her home and her bedroom, and the garden. Their paddling pool, and the trampoline. Her bike. Her iPad, and her games.

Another noise came from downstairs, and she froze. Maisie had fallen asleep, exhausted from crying most of the night.

She had to get out of here.

Tamara got to her feet quickly and went to hide beside the door. This might be her only chance.

The key was turned in the lock, and the door opened.

He stepped into the room, and she pushed him hard in his back.

As he fell forwards, she raced down the stairs, yelling for help. She had a hand on the front door, but then she was pulled away from it.

'The door is locked. Do you think I'm stupid?' He grabbed her firmly around the waist and took her back upstairs.

Tamara screamed.

'Be quiet!' he yelled.

'I want to go home.' Her cries turned to whimpers.

'Well, you can't.'

Maisie was awake now, sitting upright, a look of fright on her face.

'Why did you lie to us?' Tamara asked him as he put her down. 'You said you would take us home.'

'Shut up,' he growled.

'But you lied. Why can't we go home?'

He grabbed Tamara roughly by her arm. 'I said be quiet.'

'Ow, you're hurting me!'

'Leave my sister alone.' Maisie ran to Tamara's aid, sinking her teeth into the man's forearm.

'Why, you little...' He released Tamara and pushed Maisie away. 'Get on that bed, both of you!'

Tamara flew onto it, Maisie quickly following her. They scrambled underneath the blanket, leaving only their heads on show.

'I don't want to hear another peep out of either of you, do you hear?'

Tamara nodded, glad she'd gone to the bathroom earlier. She was so frightened now she might wet herself.

The door closed behind him, and she heard the key turn in the lock again. It wasn't fair. Why wouldn't he let them go home?

'I don't like him,' Maisie whispered. 'He's nasty.'

'Shush, he might hear you!' Tamara didn't want to think of what he might do to them if they didn't behave.

Back downstairs, he turned up the TV. Those stupid girls! They would rouse the neighbours if he wasn't careful, and that might bring someone to his door. He couldn't have that, not yet.

The older one reminded him of Holly. She was feisty, he'd give her that. The little one had a mean temper, too. He rubbed at his arm where she'd bit him. She hadn't broken his skin, but it had hurt.

Holly had always wanted to be a nurse. She would have been good at taking care of others if they were poorly. But she hadn't had the chance. Cut down in her prime.

He tried not to think about how she would be now. Twenty-eight, perhaps married with a family of her own. How could that have been taken from her? His fist curled around the can he was holding, crushing it. Then he threw it against the wall.

The news of what he'd done came on the screen again. From what he could see, it was a usual update, asking the public to look out for the missing girls.

Even spotting their parents didn't make him regret what he'd done. But then, as the bulletin ended and the next news story came on, he sat forward. His white van came into view. It was a new clip of footage from the hit-and-run on Monday night. They were searching for it, asking people for its whereabouts.

There was a bang from upstairs and crying again.

'For fuck's sake,' he seethed. He'd had enough of babysitting those brats. He marched upstairs, undid the lock, and opened the door.

'Right, get up. We're leaving.'

'Where are we going?' Tamara asked, shuffling to the edge of the bed.

'Never you mind, just hurry up.'

Tamara reached for Maisie's hand, but she shook her head.

'Come on, Maisie,' she said.

'I'm scared.'

'You'll do as you're told, or else,' he growled. 'Now, hurry up!'

CHAPTER THIRTY-NINE

Marsha was back at the station, giving her team an update of her calls that morning.

'Chris Osbourne has confirmed he was with Lucy Prophet at the family home between eight and nine on Monday morning.'

'With her as in *with* her?' Emma asked.

Marsha nodded. 'They've been having an affair.'

'But that doesn't change anything for us?' Connor concurred.

'Sadly, no,' Marsha said. 'It just rules him out and makes it more vital that he watches out for himself until we have our suspect apprehended.'

'Still, it was good to see him get punched by Dan,' Nathan said. 'He came flying into the office like the Tasmanian Devil. He was pretty furious, and I don't blame him.'

'I've located the handyman,' Emma said. 'He's coming in to give a statement. He's been in Spain for the past week, though. That's why it took him until now to come forward. I've told him to bring in confirmation details.'

'At least it will be someone off the list, seeing as we only have one person on it, and we can't even locate him.' Marsha sighed. 'I still think that the person in the white van parked at the top of Berry Lane Farm, and the footage that we got earlier of a similar vehicle seen near to the hit-and-run are connected.' She stood up. 'I think we need to take this to the press. We can get an image of Armstrong released as a person of interest, in relation to the vehicle in the hit-and-run, too. Maybe it will help to flush him out, and if so, we can rule him in or out. At the moment, we're not sure if he's involved or not. It's so frustrating.'

A few minutes later, Marsha knocked on Ryan's office door, waited for him to beckon her in, and then sat down across from him.

'Still no sign of the girls?' he asked.

'No, sir.'

'Do you think they've left the area?'

'I can't be certain.'

'Are you looking at Stephen Armstrong as a prime suspect?'

'He has to be, don't you agree?'

Ryan nodded.

'Although my first thought was that he went to attack John Prophet, and the girls and their gran got in the way.'

'What about Chris Osbourne?'

'He was, erm, seeing Dan's wife at the family home.'

Ryan raised his eyebrows and shook his head. 'Nowt as strange as folk. So has anyone got means, motive, and opportunity?'

'No, except Stephen Armstrong.'

'Do we have a recent photo of him?'

'Only one from prison two years ago. I doubt he will have changed much from then, though, except for weight and hair.'

'Okay, here's what we'll do. We can't go public with

Armstrong's name until we have more concrete evidence he's involved. At the moment—'

Marsha's phone went off. 'It's Control, sir. I need to take it.' She listened to the caller, sitting forward, eyes widening by the second. 'Copy that. I'll be right there. I'm with the DCI, so we'll get on to what's necessary.' She disconnected her phone. 'The girls have been dropped off at the newsagent's in Warren Street.'

'What?' Ryan picked up his phone. 'Go to them. I'll arrange for an ambulance to meet you there. I won't be far behind you.'

'Sir.' Marsha rang Nathan and updated him while she dashed along the corridor. 'Get my car keys and meet me downstairs. Tell Connor and Jess to come along, too.'

Marsha took the stairs as fast as her legs would carry her. So many things were running through her mind. Were the girls okay? Was it even them? She wouldn't believe it until she saw them, although who else could it be? They had clearly been recognised by the person who'd called it in.

'Are they all right?' Nathan asked when they met at her car. 'Did the caller say?'

'No, I don't have any more details, but I bloody well hope so.'

In a matter of minutes, they arrived at the newsagent's. Marsha parked up and dished out orders to Connor and Jess.

'Seal this street off at either end.' She pointed to each way. 'If it is them, why have they been dropped off here? For all we know, they could have been in a house nearby.'

She and Nathan ran inside, showing their warrant cards.

'Did you make the call, sir?' Marsha asked the man behind the counter.

'Yes.' He pointed to a door. 'They're upstairs, with my wife.'

'I'll take some details from him,' Nathan said. 'Sort out CCTV et cetera.'

Marsha nodded her thanks.

The door led to a corridor with boxes of stock the length of it. She squeezed past them, found the stairs, and took them three at a time, pulling herself up with the bannister for quickness.

She stepped inside a living area.

Sitting on the settee were Tamara and Maisie Prophet.

CHAPTER FORTY

Marsha's eyes brimmed with tears, her shoulders dropping with the relief that the girls, from the outside, seemed to be unharmed. Obviously there was going to be mental trauma after what they'd been through, and she prayed that there was nothing that she couldn't see yet, like sexual assault, that had gone on. Because why had they been set free?

The woman with them was handing a drink to Maisie, holding the cup as the little girl's hands were shaking.

Marsha kneeled down in front of them. 'Hello, girls. My name is Marsha, and I'm a police officer. This is my badge.' She reached out her warrant card and gave it to them to scrutinise. After what the girls had been through, it was imperative to gain their trust. They needed reassurance until they were reunited with their parents.

'I want you to know that you are safe here with us, and this kind lady, whose name is?'

'Becky.'

Marsha smiled at her briefly before her attention went back to Tamara and Maisie. 'Once we've seen that you're okay, we can take you to see Mummy and Daddy. Would you like that?'

Both girls nodded.

Marsha wanted to pull them into her arms, reassure them with a hug. But she held back, unsure how they would react.

'Tamara, Maisie,' she said, looking at them in turn. 'I need you to be brave as I have to ask you a few questions. Can you tell me how you got here today?'

'The man brought us,' Tamara whispered.

'Did you walk with him?'

Tamara shook her head. 'In his car.'

'That's great. Can you remember what colour it was?'

'Red.'

Red? Car? Had they been searching for the wrong vehicle? Or were there two?

'I'm going to ring your parents in a moment, Tamara, and you can speak to them on the phone until they get to you. Is that okay?'

Tamara nodded.

'Can I ask you one more thing? Do you know where you've been?'

Tamara nodded. 'I saw a street sign when he let us go. It said Western Street.'

Western Street. Where the hit-and-run had taken place.

'That's so clever of you!' Marsha encouraged. 'Did you happen to see a door number?

A shake of a head had Marsha's hopes dashed. There were over two hundred houses in Western Street.

Well, they'd just have to knock on every bloody one because she was going to hunt down whoever had done this that afternoon.

'The front door was blue,' Tamara added. 'Dark blue.'

Marsha's stomach flipped over in anticipation of the chase. She asked a few more simple questions, but Tamara clammed up. It would have to wait, probably until tomorrow, when they'd spent a night at home, in their own beds, with their parents. But what a relief it would be for all concerned to know they were safe.

'The ambulance has arrived,' Nathan said, a paramedic following him into the room.

'Hello, girls.' The woman knelt down in front of them. 'My name is Georgia. Can you tell me what your names are?'

Marsha stood up to give her some space. She slipped out of the room a couple of minutes later, leaving the girls speaking to Georgia.

When she saw Nathan, she beckoned him into the corridor.

'We've got them.' She shook her head. 'I can't believe it.'

'Me neither.' Nathan grinned, holding up a hand for her to high five. 'I really had my doubts.'

Marsha recounted what Tamara had told her. 'I'll find Ryan and see what we need to do now. But I can't wait to get them home. It's a good day, Nathan. A very good day indeed.'

Marsha spotted Ryan talking to a group of uniformed officers. He came towards her.

'That was a wonderful phone call to relay,' he said, smiling. 'I haven't given many details. How are the girls?'

'On the outside, looking good.'

They both turned their heads as a vehicle parked at the edge of the crime scene tape cordon. Marsha groaned when Max Harvey from the *Leek News* jumped out with a cameraman.

'We need to get Tamara and Maisie away from here as soon as possible,' Ryan added. 'It's too public.'

'I have a lead, sir.' Marsha relayed what Tamara had said about the car and the address. 'Shall I send some officers over to see if they can spot it?'

'Yes, straight away. Any word on Stephen Armstrong's

whereabouts?'

'No. The newsagent, Andy Wolston, said the girls walked in on their own, so they were dropped off, perhaps close to, or told where to walk to. I can talk to them more, perhaps tomorrow.'

'Yes, let's get them back home and settled before we ask them anything else.' He smiled. 'I wasn't expecting such a great result. There will be a lot of people pleased to see them, that's for sure.'

'Yes, sir. I'll give Rachel a call as soon as they're in the ambulance. I'll mention press intrusion, too, although I think they will have a job to see anything from the main road. The house is as big as Diary Croft Farm.'

He watched from behind the cordon, ensuring he stayed inconspicuous. It wasn't hard to do as there was a large crowd in front of him. People around here were so nosy.

A woman in front of him was actually filming what was going on. Hadn't they got any respect? What was happening was personal, and all she'd want to do was show the clip to everyone to say she was there. He pushed forward purposely to knock her off balance.

'Hey, watch what you're doing!' She turned to him with a scowl.

'Sorry,' he lied.

There were a bunch of officers by the entrance to the newsagent's. Some in uniform, some plainclothes. Marsha Clay was in the middle of them. He wondered what she thought about it all. He could see her, giving out orders, making sure those girls were safe. She was good at her job, he'd give her that much.

But she wasn't clever enough to outwit him. He would have his day, and probably sooner than she anticipated.

CHAPTER FORTY-ONE

While they waited for the paramedics to give the girls the all-clear, Marsha grabbed sandwiches for the team. No one would have time for a lunch break today, but she doubted anyone would be complaining.

They stood to the side of the building as uniformed officers joined them to scan the area. Marsha thought if this was Armstrong's doing, he'd probably be long gone by now. If they knew the registration number of the red car, they could put out an alert so it would ping up on ANPR. She was hoping that someone in the vicinity would have footage of it.

A few minutes later, food had been wolfed down and drinks were drunk. Marsha saw the paramedic from earlier coming towards them.

'They look fine,' Georgia said.

'Oh, that's a relief.' Marsha's shoulders sagged as she relaxed a little.

'Obviously, I'm not qualified to check them over for everything, but from the questions I asked and their outward appearance, they're good to go.'

'Thanks. I'm sure the parents will take them to their local

GP if there are any concerns. Best leave that to them. Those girls have been through enough. What questions did you ask them?'

'I tried to keep to the basics, just enough to see if they were hurt. Maisie didn't say anything, but Tamara said they were locked in a room in a house. A man brought in food and let them use the bathroom.'

Marsha shuddered involuntarily, thankful that they were in one piece. She looked at Jess who had joined her.

'Can you call Rachel and let her know we're coming?'

'Yes, boss.'

Marsha held her face up to the sun for a moment, trying to hold in her emotion. Tonight, she was sure she'd shed a few tears, but for now, she had to stay professional. And the girls were safe.

Fifteen minutes later, with the children in the rear seat, Marsha turned into the drive of the Prophet home.

'I can't believe we're doing this,' Jess said quietly. 'It's such a good outcome.'

Marsha nodded. It would have been better if they'd apprehended a suspect at the same time, but there was always tomorrow. First thing in the morning, she'd be back to speak to Tamara, to see if she could shed any light on who had held them captive.

Because if it was Armstrong, he would know they'd be on to him now they had the girls. She couldn't understand what his game was.

'There's Mummy and Daddy!' Maisie cried, waving frantically.

Marsha saw Dan and Lucy run towards the vehicle, Rachel hanging back behind them. Even before the engine was killed, they were opening the rear doors and grabbing a girl apiece.

Tears poured down their faces as they embraced their

children, and both Jess and Marsha struggled to hold in their emotions.

They went inside and, when the girls ran into the kitchen, Marsha caught up with their parents.

'They seem to be fine,' she said. 'Obviously, they'll speak to you more about their ordeal, but I'd like to visit in the morning and show Tamara a few photos to see if she can spot who held them captive.'

'If I get my hands on that...bastard.' Dan shook his head. 'Do you know if it was him? Armstrong?'

'It's too soon to tell.'

'But he needs to be caught. Why haven't you got him yet?'

'It's inevitable you'll be angry. There's always a feeling of inadequacy in situations such as these, mainly because often there isn't a good outcome,' Marsha explained. 'So once they're resolved, it's as if all the emotions come at once. Take your time letting everything out. It will hit you more later, that they are safe now.'

'And no one...' Lucy stopped. 'Did he... anyone touch them?'

'We don't think so, but again, it will be best coming from you asking the awkward questions to figure that out. For now, they seem happy to be home. We did think of taking them to hospital, but they might have been there for hours, and we thought it best to get them in familiar surroundings. However, if you want to take them, Rachel will go with you.'

They could hear chatter coming from the kitchen, Maisie giggling. It was so wonderful to hear.

'We'll see if our GP will visit.' Dan offered his hand. 'Thank you. I wasn't sure we'd... well, you know. But they're back.'

'We'll also need to take their clothes and shoes, for evidence. They will be useful for us to link to when we find out where they were held.'

'Yes, of course.' Lucy nodded. 'I'll get them changed now.'

Thank you.' Marsha stopped. 'I'm sorry we lost your father, Dan. How's Sylvia?'

'She might be out tomorrow, if not, the day after for certain. She'll be glad to hear we have the girls home.'

'Please send her my regards.' Marsha smiled. 'I think we can leave you to it now. Rachel will be on hand until you need her. And I'm sure the press will be camped out soon, so perhaps you'd be better staying in the rear of the house for now. Or in a hotel if you prefer? We can arrange one for you if so.'

'No, we're fine here.' Dan's face broke out into a tentative smile.

'We'll be giving an update soon. There's obviously no need for you to join us now. Locally, I expect the news will be out. We can't stop social media exploding after what's happened this afternoon.'

'I don't care who knows, as long as they're back. After you called Rachel to say they were on their way home, I rang the office to let everyone know. I hope that was okay.'

'Absolutely fine.'

A message came through on Marsha's phone. She quickly scanned it. 'We need to go. Rachel will be with you for now, and we'll keep in touch.'

'Thank you so much,' Lucy said, clearly overwhelmed by everything.

They got back into the car, and Marsha turned to Jess. 'They've found the house in Western Street.'

CHAPTER FORTY-TWO

Having waited for a search warrant to be issued for number eighteen Western Street, Marsha had sent Connor and Nathan ahead. Now, she parked outside a cordon that had been placed either side of the house.

She and Jess produced their warrant cards, signed the log book, and made their way to the property. Marsha kept her eyes peeled for cameras but couldn't see any personal CCTV.

The house was the end one in a block of four. There was just enough room to park a car in the drive, and a postage-stamp-sized lawn beside it, overgrown and littered with detritus.

The blue front door was now looking worse for wear as the Enforcer had been used to gain entry.

Nathan was outside talking to one of the officers. As soon as he spotted them, he met them at the kerb.

'The place is clear, boss,' he said. 'No sign of Armstrong, but it's definitely the right house. Close neighbours have described him, said he lives alone. Uniform have started house-to-house, and Connor is inside. I'm going to join him unless you need me to do anything else?'

'No, come on in when you're done here.' Marsha raised her eyebrows at Jess as they slipped on gloves and shoe covers. 'Good old Detective Tamara.'

They stepped inside a hallway, with stairs leading off it. Ahead was a kitchen, to the right a living room. The property was small, so she surmised two bedrooms upstairs.

They went into the galley kitchen first. It was a block of white units either side, the worktops piled high with food, dirty dishes, and a stash of empty beer cans and bottles of vodka. She put a hand to the side of the kettle: the water inside was cold.

She opened the fridge to find half a bottle of milk, a packet of cheese squares, and a tub of butter.

'Grimy, isn't it, boss?' Jess opened a wall cupboard and moved her head away from the stench, closing it quickly.

'Disgusting,' Marsha muttered, pulling her foot away from the floor covering, where it was stuck in a sticky patch of goodness knows what. She grimaced.

Through a vestibule was a downstairs toilet that she didn't wish to stay near for too long.

They found Connor in the living room. The curtains were across, so she drew them open slightly, enough to let in a little light but also maintaining their privacy. Dust motes bobbed about, and she coughed slightly.

It wasn't a pretty sight. There was a TV unit with a drawer, and a sideboard behind a two seater settee. On the wall were a few family photos. One in particular caught her eye.

Two teenage boys were standing on her favourite spot at the top of The Roaches, arms around each other and punching the air. Next to them was a younger girl, holding a toddler.

Was this the Armstrong kids? If so, they seemed so close

back then. Marsha and her brother, Joe, had been like that. God, how she missed him at times like these.

Life could be so cruel. They looked as if they were having fun, sharing a happy childhood. Who would have thought that a few years later, everything would change through one reckless act?

The family had been tarnished, heartbroken by the loss of Holly, then wrecked when Stephen had gone to prison because of what he'd done. A whole lifetime of memories fractured in a single second. It was unbearable to see, because she'd felt that way about her life. A shiver ran down her spine.

Jess had gone upstairs. Walking up to her, Marsha was thankful she wouldn't have to step into the bathroom she could see through its open door.

It was as grubby as the kitchen, the white suite having seen better days, and there was a musty smell which made her wrinkle up her nose.

A few toiletries stood in a row along the windowsill. One toothbrush lay on the sink.

'He might have kept Tamara and Maisie in here, but I can't see any signs of them,' Jess said, pointing to the bedroom door. 'These are really ancient, and there's an old-fashioned lock in the handle. It feels like a room that wasn't in use.'

'We'll get forensics to rip it apart.'

'There's some stuff you'll want to see in the room at the front, though.'

Marsha followed Jess into it. The double bed was unmade, the duvet overturned enough to let a person roll out of it. The smell was sour in here, too, sweaty feet and unwashed skin. But it was what was on the old dressing table that drew her attention.

Paper cuttings from the *Leek News* with every mention of the Prophet family.

'Bingo,' Marsha muttered.

She flicked through them: one of John Prophet handing over the keys to Dan when he retired, one of Dan and his daughters at a summer fair. Another of the garage forecourt. There was even a piece about her, giving out an award to John Prophet last month.

'He's been planning this for months, years even, by the looks of things,' she said. 'I wonder what the trigger was to act now. The anniversary of her death, do you think?'

'It's more than likely. There's not much else in here to go on.' Jess was now rifling through a set of drawers. 'There's a bag over there with a few clothes in it. It's as if he never unpacked.'

'Perhaps why he hasn't registered on the electoral roll.'

'Mind you, who'd want to live here?' Jess picked up a pair of jeans between two fingers to search the pockets. 'It's the pits.'

'All I want is the knife that was used to kill John Prophet.'

'He could have stashed that anywhere. It might not even be in here.'

'I know that, but humour me.'

They shared a smile.

Searching around for a few more minutes and finding nothing important, Marsha called it a day. 'We'll leave the rest to the search and forensic teams. I'm sure, with more time, they'll find something for us.'

'Boss,' Nathan shouted up to her. 'Uniform has found the white van.'

Marsha hung her head over the bannister. 'Where?'

'Down by the park, on a garage plot. It's burned out.'

'So the likelihood of us getting prints is minus nothing.' She rolled her eyes. 'You win some, you lose some. Go and check it out anyway. I'll leave Jess here with Connor and go back to the station to regroup.'

CHAPTER FORTY-THREE

It was half past nine. After an exciting day, the evening fell flat. Like Marsha had presumed, the burned-out van had yielded nothing so far, and was unlikely to either. Both number plates had been removed before it was set alight.

There were no vehicles registered at eighteen Western Street, so they didn't know the details of the red car, but neighbours said it was a 2015 Ford Fiesta. No one had seen it there for a few days, which meant Armstrong must have somewhere else to park it or store it out of sight, or it too had been abandoned and they hadn't found it yet.

Marsha had been to see Ryan who'd refused to give details out to the press that Stephen Armstrong was a person of interest. She'd gone head-to-head with him, but he hadn't budged.

'We don't have any evidence to give out his name,' he said. 'We have a burned-out white van with no prints.'

'We're searching for the red Fiesta now.'

'The van may or may not be the same vehicle seen around Dairy Croft Farm. We have a photo that he's on, and we're working on the assumption he's the one who is getting at the others. For all we know, Armstrong could be dead somewhere, and someone else is killing everyone in that photo.'

'You know that's unlikely.'

'I do, but it is possible. We don't have anything that puts him at either crime scene. A few newspaper cuttings, and a house Tamara and Maisie may have stayed in isn't enough, yet. If forensics can confirm the girls were there, then yes, we could proceed.'

'We don't need evidence just to talk to him, sir,' Marsha retorted.

'*You* don't need to tell me that. But look at what would happen if we got it wrong.'

'We haven't got—'

'I know.' He held up a hand. 'But imagine how he might get hounded on social media.'

Marsha had to concede Ryan was right.

'Wait until you've spoken to Tamara Prophet. If she identifies Armstrong, then we'll go to the press immediately.'

'Isn't that the same as having no concrete evidence, the word of an eight-year-old?'

'Yes, but good enough if linked to forensic evidence that they were held in Western Street. It's frustrating, but you need to be patient, Marsha.'

'Yes, sir.' Her voice was flat. 'I know you're right. I just have a feeling that he won't be going back there, and I really want to nail the bastard.'

'Marsha, you've had a great day!'

She rubbed at her aching neck.

'So get yourself off to the pub for a quick one. Boost morale.'

She smirked as she left his office.

Back in her own, she sensed the trauma of the day was setting in, taking everything out of them.

'Anyone fancy a drink before home?' Marsha asked.

'Not for me,' Connor said. 'I fancy seeing the kids before they're in bed.'

'Aw, you softie,' Marsha teased.

'Not for me either.' Jess glanced up from her computer screen. 'I want more than a lemonade. There's a glass of wine with my name on it in the fridge at my mum's.'

'I'm going to take a rain check, too, as I'm into overtime.' Emma reached for her handbag, searching out her car keys.

'Party poopers, the lot of you,' Marsha jested. She turned to Nathan who had just come back into the room. 'Pub, Nath? My shout?'

'Sure,' Nathan said.

They said their goodbyes in the car park and, when they were inside The Jug, Marsha went to the bar while Nathan grabbed a table. Once settled, they chatted for a few minutes.

'Do you want another?' she asked when she noticed Nathan had downed most of his pint. As she'd had a G and T, her drink was gone, too.

'It's my round.'

'No, my treat.'

'Go on then, cheers.' He grinned. 'The best thing about living in the town you're working in is that you don't always bring your car.'

Marsha fetched another round. She slid Nathan's drink across the table and sat down again. 'There you go.'

'Cheers.'

But, after necking the first pint down quickly, it was almost as if Nathan then stopped. He stared down into his glass.

'Are you okay?' Marsha enquired. 'It's not like you to snap at a new member of staff, like you did with Jess on Monday. Has your nose been pushed out of joint because you don't get to hang around with Connor now? It's not all boys together?'

Nathan screwed up his face. 'I was out of order with Jess.'

'Not me you should be saying that to. She's trying to settle in, find her place, and you're putting her on edge.'

'Sorry, I'll sort it.'

'And there's nothing else?' Marsha probed, convinced there was. Nathan wouldn't let anything so trivial get him down.

'Apart from me being a bloody fool?' He huffed. 'It's... me and Amy have split up.'

CHAPTER FORTY-FOUR

Marsha's eyes widened in astonishment. She hadn't been expecting that.

'It was my fault,' Nathan went on. 'One bloody moment of madness. I was on a night out with the lads. Before leaving the house, me and Amy had a huge row, and I was smarting from it. I was pretty angry and had too much to drink. Then I saw this girl I'd had a crush on at school.'

'Oh dear.' Marsha grimaced, guessing at where the conversation was going.

'It had never been reciprocated. I don't think she even knew I existed back then. But we went to the bar at the same time, got chatting and... ended up leaving together.'

'Nathan!' Marsha couldn't help herself. 'You didn't.'

'I did. I woke up in her flat, in her bed, around three a.m. I was bloody mortified and jumped in a taxi. When I got up the next morning, I acted like nothing had happened. But I felt so guilty. Eventually, I told Connor about it.'

'You couldn't confide in me?' Marsha was hurt.

'I was too embarrassed.'

'What did he say?'

'He told me I was a stupid idiot but to chalk it down to experience and, under no circumstances, mention it to Amy.'

She paused. 'So I'd say you couldn't live with yourself, and you told her?'

Nathan nodded. 'It was making me ill. I couldn't concentrate when I was at work, and I felt so guilty when I was at home. I wasn't sleeping. So, two weeks later, I confessed.' He snorted. 'I'd hoped that after a frank discussion about why I'd found the need to sleep with someone else, we might have been able to move forwards, start talking things through. But Connor was right. It had been a mistake to say anything. A *huge* mistake, and I only had myself to blame.'

'But there must have been something wrong in your relationship for you to act like you did? You're not an insincere prick who can't keep it in his pants.'

He smiled at that. 'I just felt like we were drifting. I know the job is demanding when a major crime comes in, yet most of the time it's sensible hours. But I felt like we were starting to live like brother and sister. We'd only been married for six years. I guess I wanted some excitement again. Although I sure pick my moments.'

'What did Amy say?'

'She hit the roof and threw me out on the spot. I had to go home to my parents with my tail between my legs, praying she'd calm down. But she didn't.'

A couple came in hand in hand. Marsha and Nathan watched as they looked around for a spare table and went towards it, not letting go of each other. It was clear they were in the lust stage of their romance.

Marsha rolled her eyes at Nathan discreetly. 'It can't always be like that. Life gets in the way.'

'I'm not proud of what I did,' Nathan added. 'I hurt Amy deeply, and I miss her like crazy, I'd do anything for her to forgive me, but it's been three months now. I'm living with my olds – not liking that at all – so I need to find a flat. I still hope she'll want me back eventually.'

'How did Daisy take it?'

'She's been fine, really, but Amy had been using her as a pawn to get back at me. I miss them both desperately, yet Amy makes it difficult for me to see Daisy.'

'She denies you access?'

'Not as such. She just changes her plans at the last minute, saying Daisy will be going somewhere with her instead. I'm hoping she stops doing it soon. The only person it's hurting is our little girl.'

'Wow.' Marsha was stunned. 'That's quite some story. I can't believe you haven't told me about it. I'm your friend as well as your line manager.'

'You don't think any less of me for sleeping around?'

He was ashamed, but at the same time, it seemed Marsha's opinion was important to him.

'That's none of my business. But I'm here if you want to talk anytime.' She pointed at his pint. 'I think you need to leave that where it is, before you order more and get so drunk you'll regret it in the morning.'

'Like the last time?' He pushed the glass away. 'Don't think I'll ever be up for that again.'

Marsha sighed as she walked along Derby Street. People, they all had problems, either of their own making or someone else's.

She couldn't believe that Nathan and Amy's marriage was in trouble, too. Well, it could actually be over already.

She'd always got on with Amy, teasing Nathan that he wasn't good enough for her. They suited each other.

What an idiot he'd been. She hoped they'd be able to patch things up. Having said that, she wasn't sure how she'd feel about Phil if she found out he'd been sleeping with someone else.

Nathan would be lost without Amy, though. She remembered their wedding. They had been so in love, and when Daisy had come along it had been the icing on the cake.

Yet, she knew, only too well, that being a police officer took its toll on relationships. With long hours working murder cases or being on call and having to cancel things last minute, resentment often built up. Not to mention the many work affairs because people were there more than they were at home.

As soon as Marsha got in, Larry bounded towards her.

'Let me get the key out of the door,' she laughed as he jumped up to greet her. She listened for a moment, but there was silence. 'Anyone home?' she shouted.

There was no reply.

'It's just you and me again, kiddo.' She stroked Larry's head. 'So I'm going to make the most of it.'

CHAPTER FORTY-FIVE

He sat in his car outside Chris Osbourne's house. It was easy to fit in unnoticed in a line of parked vehicles along the road. Osbourne lived in a semi-detached house, with a garage, and a BMW parked on the drive.

It was late, and no one had gone in or out for the past two hours.

The can of petrol was in the well of the passenger seat, full to the brim. Knowing he'd be captured on CCTV, he'd filled it up a few weeks ago, paying by cash so there was no paper trail.

The street was busy for the time of night, and he'd gone to get out of his car twice and been interrupted. He wondered if it was worth waiting around, or doing what he needed to before the heat was on him.

He laughed at his thoughts.

Heat would certainly be on someone.

He couldn't get close enough to kill Osbourne now. The police would be after him, he was sure, so he had to try and stay one step ahead for as long as he could. He wouldn't be surprised if there were officers in the house, waiting for him to strike. He wasn't that stupid.

But he did want to burn his house down to the ground. Show Osbourne what it felt like to lose everything. Because, from what he'd been told, it was Osbourne who had started it all.

The accident had changed his family overnight. His mother had been vilified in the street for not looking after Holly properly, which was so wrong. Most of her friends and neighbours hadn't spoken to her anymore, not even to say hello as they'd walked past. Well, some did, but they'd stared and snarled, blaming her for what had happened.

As well as losing his younger sister, the prettiest girl with a bright future ahead of her, his father turned into a monster. To most people outside the home, Edwin was still the same. But he started drinking heavily. He couldn't take the grief that Holly had gone and would come home from the pub and take it out on anyone who was there.

He got out of the house as soon as he could after that. Getting married had been a mistake because he was so screwed up himself, but at least they'd had two great kids together. That's when he'd understood the love he'd lost from Edwin and how much he wanted it back.

When his mum had died, all he'd longed to hear his dad say again was that he loved him. He wasn't perfect, far from it. But he was Edwin's son.

A car door slamming a few metres in front brought him to his senses. He started the engine and pulled away from the kerb.

His killing spree was over. He'd failed in his full mission, but at least he could do some damage before he left. It was time for plan B.

It was good the police didn't know he had the Fiesta, and even if they did, the number plates on it weren't the right ones. Still, he drove slowly through the backstreets to get to Prophet and Sons.

By now, it was midnight and quieter. He wasn't bothered about being seen or picked up on camera at this stage, but he didn't want anyone to stop him.

He came in at the back of the garage and parked at the top of Springfield Road. Then he put on a baseball cap, picked up his can, and set off.

The lights were bright on the forecourt. He waited for two cars to drive past and then jogged across to the reception. Deftly, he opened the letter box on the main door and poured petrol in. Next, he lit a match and, with a satisfying look at the camera above his head, flicked it through the gap.

A ball of flames rose. He stepped away, in case the glass burst before he had time to get away.

He watched for a few seconds and then went back to his car. He drove away quickly now, hoping to stay hidden for the night.

He didn't have much time, but he had to see his dad once more, and then he'd be leaving for good.

CHAPTER FORTY-SIX

Thursday

Marsha woke up with a start. Surprisingly, she'd slept well that night, perhaps comforted knowing Tamara and Maisie Prophet would have been safely tucked up in their beds.

She cast her mind back to yesterday, the relief on Dan and Lucy Prophets' faces when they'd taken the girls home. Despite Phil not being enamoured with her job, Marsha was good at it. She loved it, lived for it, even. She wouldn't apologise to him for that.

Today, though, there was still a killer out there. They had to find Stephen Armstrong and talk to him. It would be her job to coax as much information from Tamara Prophet this morning as she could.

If Tamara identified Stephen from a photo, then they could go public with it. People had to be warned about him, and they needed to get him in a cell.

Marsha wondered how Dan and Lucy were faring. She'd noticed they'd been cold with each other, obviously bruised by news of the affair coming to light. Maybe their girls would get them through the worst now. Putting on a brave face for children more often than not didn't work out in a troubled marriage, but these were unusual circumstances.

Phil yawned loudly and turned to face her. She groaned inwardly, not wanting that chat yet.

'Morning,' he said.

'Hey. What time did you come in last night?'

'About half eleven. Went for a drink after work. Well done on finding those girls. It must be a relief.'

'It is. Just need to catch who did it and then solve the rest of the case now.'

Phil's smile was faint. He went to speak again but at the last minute seemed to change his mind. Instead, he drew back the duvet and left the room.

Marsha sighed, stretching her hands above her head. She could hear him in the bathroom. There had been times when she'd have sneaked in and joined him in the shower before going to work. They hadn't done that in a long time. Did she even want to anymore?

She sighed dramatically. This couldn't go on for much longer. She would talk to him once this case was over.

Downstairs, Larry thumped his tail on the floor, unable, it seemed, to get out of his bed. It was obvious he'd been let out into the garden. Usually, he'd be dancing at the door by now.

'Hey, big fella,' she said, stooping next to him to ruffle his ears. His look of sheer adoration cheered her up immensely.

Cassie was already at the kitchen table, her head in a text book.

'You're up early today. Last-minute revision?'

Cassie nodded. 'English Lit, and then I am done. At midday, I will be a free woman, and I can't wait.'

Marsha bent forward and gave her a hug. 'I'm proud of

you for knuckling down. These are the most important exams you'll take. They can lead you on to so many things.'

'It's not *that* I'm revising hard for. It's because you promised me twenty quid for every one I pass, plus a meal out wherever I want to go.'

Marsha laughed, not having an answer for that.

'Best of luck, kiddo.' She waved as she left for work.

The first thing she heard about when she arrived was the fire overnight at Prophet and Son. She sent Nathan to investigate. Connor was clearing outstanding actions, and she wanted him in the office with Emma, in readiness to man the phones once she'd given Ryan the go-ahead.

An hour later, Marsha and Jess were at the Prophet home.

'How was everyone yesterday, after we'd left?' Marsha asked, once they were seated in the lounge.

Lucy had made coffee and provided a plate of pastries. The coffee was welcome, but Marsha declined the sweet treat. She couldn't speak and eat one of those without making a mess.

'The girls were really well, actually,' Lucy said. 'It was Dan and I who were in bits. We held it together until they were in bed, and then we bawled like babies.'

Dan smiled then. It was only the second time Marsha had seen him do that this week.

'Tamara was a bit subdued, I guess with her being older,' Lucy went on. 'But Maisie was just glad to be reunited with her toys and iPad. She was soon settled, just as if she'd been on holiday for a few nights.'

'I'm sorry to hear about the fire last night. Was there much damage?'

Dan shook his head. 'Most of the reception area is a mess, but luckily, as the doors were closed through to the rest of the building, it was limited to that room. Do you think it was

Armstrong? It's a bit of a coincidence that it happened once we got the girls home.'

'We're looking into that possibility,' Marsha said. 'One of my officers has gone straight there this morning.'

'I left details with Sarah, so he can check the CCTV. I was knackered last night.'

'That's fine. Hopefully, we can capture the culprit on film.'

'I bloody hope so.'

'I wanted to ask if you'd let me speak to Tamara, with you present, of course. We need to see if she can recognise the man, who we believe to be Stephen Armstrong. Without anyone seeing him, we only have circumstantial evidence, and not enough to give out his name to the public.'

Both Dan and Lucy had remained quiet, so Marsha continued.

'I have several photos, with his among them, that I would like to show to her.'

'I don't think she's ready,' Lucy said. 'It's too soon.'

'I understand, but we need to catch who is responsible for this, and for what they did to John and Sylvia. I promise I won't be more than a few minutes, and if I see her getting distressed, I'll stop.'

Dan nodded slightly at Lucy, and she stood up.

'I'll fetch her for you.'

'I'll come with you,' Jess said. 'I'd like to see Maisie. I won't ask her anything, but she may volunteer information, and we can talk to her later, if necessary.'

Marsha liked that Jess had used her initiative.

She and Dan were left alone, and she felt a comfortable silence fall between them. It had obviously been good for him to get his girls home safely. It would be for anyone, but at least there was no hostility.

It was her job to tease as much detail as she could from Tamara now. Dan needed closure for his parents, too.

'Thanks for this, Dan,' she said. 'Tamara is our only witness, well, apart from Maisie.'

'If it helps catch whoever did this, I'm all for it. We'll take care of Tam afterwards.'

The young girl came into the room, holding Lucy's hand. She seemed refreshed and carefree, as if the troubles of the past few days had been washed away with a shower.

Marsha imagined she'd be clingy for a while, Maisie, too. Perhaps once they were back at school, and in their regular routine again, they might be able to heal from their trauma. Their family life was enviable, one of wealth to cushion the blow. It didn't work out that way for most victims.

Marsha waited while they sat down. And then she began.

CHAPTER FORTY-SEVEN

'Hi, Tamara, how are you today?' Marsha asked the young girl.

'Okay, thank you,' Tamara replied, her eyes wary.

'Could I talk to you about what happened before you returned home yesterday?'

There was a shrug, and Marsha smiled encouragingly.

'I promise I won't be long, but I think anything you can tell us might help the police find who did this to you and Maisie, and to your grandparents. Can you tell me what happened when you first saw the man?'

Tamara sat quietly for a moment, as if she wasn't able to say any words, and then she spoke.

'Someone had hurt Granddad and Gran, and he told us he had come to help. He was holding Granddad, and he was falling to the floor. Gran was over by the wall, and there was blood on her head. I looked at her, and he told me to keep my eyes on him.'

'That's very good, Tamara,' Marsha encouraged. 'What happened then?'

'He said he would take us to the police. I didn't want to go with him at first. I wanted to stay with Gran and Granddad.'

She glanced at her parents with a guilty expression. 'But he said to hurry in case the man who attacked them came back. He took us to his car, and we got in. He told us to be quiet and not to be afraid.'

'And did he take you to the house in Western Street then?'

Tamara nodded. 'He made us go upstairs into a bedroom and hide. And then he locked the door. We were frightened.'

Marsha's temper rose. One hour with whoever had done this in a room, that's all she asked for, and she would make sure they wouldn't be fit to commit another crime.

She took a deep breath to rid herself of silly thoughts and continued.

'Can you tell me about the room you were in?'

'It was smelly and dusty. There wasn't much furniture. A bed, like mine and Maisie's, not as big as Mum and Dad's, and a wardrobe, but there was nothing inside it.'

That seemed to tally with what they'd seen at number eighteen yesterday. 'And was the man nasty to you?'

Tamara nodded. 'He shouted at us, told us to be quiet. But Maisie kept crying. He said the neighbours would hear.'

'He didn't hurt you?'

'Not really.'

'What do you mean?' Dan interrupted.

'I tried to escape when he came into the room, but he grabbed my arm. Maisie bit him.'

Dan smiled at that.

'He brought us food, and sweets and drinks, and he let us use the bathroom.' Tamara screwed up her face. 'That was disgusting.'

Marsha thanked the Lord for small mercies. It seemed that all they might have gone through was being locked in a room together, no abuse, except for the mental pressures extolled through fear and fright. She was glad the girls had been together.

A message came through on her phone. She read it quickly before continuing.

'One last thing, and then we're all done. I'm sure you can't wait to join Maisie out in the garden again.' Marsha got out her iPad and opened it at a collage of six photos Emma had collated for her. 'I've brought some pictures with me. If you can see the man who took you to his house, can you point to him, please? It would be very helpful.'

Tamara glanced up at her mum, panic in her eyes.

'It's okay,' Lucy soothed. 'You don't have to, but I think you should, Tam, because you'd be helping to catch him. The police need to know what he looks like, and Gran can't remember much. Can you be brave?'

'Okay.' Tamara nodded.

Marsha leaned across, holding on to the iPad, and showed the images to the young girl.

Tamara viewed them for a few seconds, and when her gaze fell on one man she burst into tears. Then she hid her face in her mum's chest.

'Is the man in the photo, Tamara?' Marsha asked gently.

'Of course he is,' Dan cried. 'You only have to see her reaction.'

'I'm sorry, but I need confirmation,' Marsha told him, turning back to his daughter. 'Tamara?'

'It's him. It's him. It's him,' Tamara cried. 'Mummy, I don't want to see him.'

'Okay, we can leave it there for now, sweetheart.' Marsha waited until Tamara, caught her eye. 'But I want you to know that the information you have given to us has been vital for our investigation. What you have done is so brave. I believe you took care of Maisie well, too. You are a strong girl, and your parents are very proud of you.'

Tamara, who had stopped crying now, nodded and sniffed.

'So, can I ask you to point at who it was? You have my word that I won't ask you anything else.'

Tamara pointed to the image of Stephen Armstrong and then hid her face again.

Marsha went to call Ryan while everyone went back into the garden.

'DCI Dixon.'

'It's Marsha, sir. We have a positive ID on Stephen Armstrong.'

'You're absolutely sure?'

'After witnessing Tamara's reaction, yes, sir. I'm sure. Plus Nathan has messaged me. He has camera footage of him setting fire to the garage last night.'

'Okay. We're all set here. The press release will be live and shared in approximately thirty minutes.'

'Shall I get uniform to pick up Chris Osbourne, bring him to the station, just to be sure? Especially after the fire.'

'Yes. Armstrong could well be out of the county by now, but until we locate him, I think it's the safest thing to do.'

Marsha joined Jess in the garden then, watching Maisie for a few minutes before they left. Tamara had been extremely brave, and the family needed privacy, and time to heal.

And they had a killer to catch.

CHAPTER FORTY-EIGHT

Janine Toole was in a foul mood as she did her rounds that morning. Her son had come in from his friend's house the night before and left the place like a tip. Not only that, but he'd eaten the bread that she was going to use for her sandwiches and finished the milk she needed for her breakfast.

Why did teenagers think it was okay to eat their parents out of house and home? It was bad enough that she was a single mum, struggling with the finances, and depressed about being on her own for so long after her husband, Paul, had died. At least she only had Ollie. Thank goodness she didn't have two teenagers at home.

He was a good lad, really, apart from his mountainous appetite. He'd grown into the image of his father, and just as tall. Sixteen, and already she knew he was going to break hearts.

He wanted to join the police force once he was old enough. It was something that bothered her immensely. Working on the streets was a dangerous job and had got worse through the years. Yet equally, it made her proud that he wanted a career helping others.

On the second floor, she knocked and went into the first of sixteen rooms. 'Morning, Iris, my love. How are you today?'

'I'm a bit sore from my operation the other day, but other than that, I'm grand.' Her smile was wide, showing a set of crooked teeth. 'How are you?'

'Oh, I'm good, thank you.' Janine grinned. It wasn't often anyone asked after her. Iris was a tonic and, by the time Janine left the room twenty minutes later, her mood had lifted, and she was back to her normal self.

She checked her watch to see she was due a break soon. There were only two more patients to check in with. She would see to them, and then go downstairs to the staffroom to fetch her purse. It would have to be a shop-bought something or other to eat now.

'Hi, Edwin,' she said, rapping on the open door before going in.

'Hello.' Edwin coughed violently.

Janine rushed to sit him forward, fluffing his pillows, hoping that would ease his pain. She'd been looking after him for two weeks now. He was on palliative care, getting worse each day.

As she did with all the patients when they first came to Blue Meadows Hospice, she'd made time to get to know him, chatting to him as long as he was able to enjoy her company. It made for a better day all round. It was always sad when one of the patients passed away.

The news was showing on the TV. As she refilled Edwin's water jug, her eyes were drawn to the man whose image filled the screen. She did a double-take.

There, larger than life, was Edwin's son.

Surreptitiously, she caught snippets of what the presenter was saying.

Police are appealing for thirty-four-year-old Stephen Armstrong to come forward as he is wanted in connection with the murder of

John Prophet, the attack on his wife, Sylvia, and for abducting Tamara and Maisie Prophet.'

Janice gasped. What the hell?

'Tamara and Maisie had been missing since Monday morning but were found safe and well after walking into Wolston's Newsagent's, Leek, Staffordshire.'

She couldn't believe she'd been in the same room as a murderer!

'Police are urging the public not to approach Mr Armstrong, but to call them as soon as possible.'

Embarrassed for Edwin, Janine turned away from him. She didn't know what to say anyway. Instead, she made an excuse and moved towards the door.

'They've got it wrong,' Edwin whispered.

It was so faint that Janine almost missed it. But she kept on going, pretending that she hadn't heard him.

In the corridor, she took out her phone and dialled 999. She was through to the local police in less than a minute.

Chris Osbourne sat in the rear of the police car. Although he was annoyed that he needed to leave his home, he was glad he would feel safe soon.

He hadn't slept well since Monday, wondering and worrying if whoever was doing the killings would come after him. He could look after himself in a fist fight, but knives and cars were a whole different ball game.

He was so glad to hear that Tamara and Maisie were back at home, and safe and well by all accounts. Hearing about the fire had shocked him, too. Could it really be all of Stephen Armstrong's doing?

He couldn't help thinking back to the time when Steve had been employed at the garage. Steve had been sixteen, he and Dan nineteen. Steve had been the lacky lad. It was always the case that the youngest, or last one in, got to do the things no one else wanted to do. They were the butt of everyone's jokes and made to do some terrible forfeits and tasks.

Steve had been easy to wind up. One day, they'd travelled to Buxton to collect a car part that was needed immediately. Driving back to Leek, Chris had put his foot down and frightened the life out of Steve.

The young lad had almost burst into tears, hanging on for dear life when Chris had flown down Solomon's Hollow and then up the other side.

Yet, once it had been over, Steve had laughed it off.

It had been the following month that the accident happened, not long after Steve had passed his driving test. Chris was convinced that Steve had been showing off with his sister and lost control. Holly wouldn't have stood a chance when the car lost control, hit a stone wall, and then rolled over several times, finally landing on its roof.

If he recalled correctly, Steve had come away with a broken arm and collarbone. His family had disintegrated, though. Edwin had left Prophet and Son shortly after the fight with John Prophet.

The atmosphere at work had been hard to stomach until things started to fade. And yet, now it seemed as if Stephen Armstrong was taking revenge for what had happened, when it had been his fault. He was obviously twisted to do what he'd done.

Or maybe he blamed them all in a way. Perhaps that was why he was coming after them all now.

The officer who had picked him up was PC Seb Hadley. He took him around the back of the police station, through the security gates, and into the rear of the building.

'Sorry we can't put you anywhere else, but if we haven't caught him by tomorrow, we can arrange a hotel with a guard,' Seb said.

'It's fine,' Chris said. 'I'm just happy to be out of danger. I can't believe Steve is doing this.'

'He's a troubled fella, all right.' Seb pressed his lanyard to the pad and was buzzed in. 'We're doing our best to apprehend him as soon as possible.'

'Do you think he's left the area? I know I would. I'd be out of here like a shot.'

'We're looking into it,' was all the officer would commit to.

Fifteen minutes later, Chris was in a soft interview room. The door was closed, and he could leave to use the bathroom, but other than that, he was told to stay put.

He ran a hand through his hair and thought about Stephen Armstrong. He would have been sitting in a cell, unable to get out, knowing that his sister was dead, and that it was his fault.

What a week. Not only had Chris lost some dear friends, his relationship with the woman he loved was over, and there was no chance of being made a partner in the garage.

He had nothing. Kind of apt, he thought, considering.

CHAPTER FORTY-NINE

Marsha was back at the station with Jess. Emma had been showing her the CCTV she'd found of the red Fiesta they assumed belonged to Stephen Armstrong. She had also viewed the footage of the suspect pouring petrol into the door of Prophet and Son and running away as it caught fire. It was definitely Stephen Armstrong.

She gulped down half a mug of lukewarm coffee with a grimace, as a call came through from control. Someone from Blue Meadow Hospice had news of Armstrong. Grabbing her bag and keys again, she relayed the information to Jess.

'Do you think this is the breakthrough we need, boss?' Jess asked as they sped out of the car park.

'I hope so. Things will have to start slotting into place soon.'

Within fifteen minutes, they were parked up and with care worker, Janine Toole, and the manager of the hospice, Sadie Peters, in a side room.

At a guess, Sadie was in her late fifties. She wore her blonde hair in a ponytail, red-framed glasses matching the colour of her lipstick.

'He was here.' Janine pointed to her phone where the image of Stephen Armstrong was on display. 'He's been every afternoon this week to see his father. Edwin is in palliative care. He hasn't got long to live at all.'

Marsha's stomach flipped over. 'What time does he usually come?'

'After lunch. He only stays for a few minutes because Edwin is so tired.' Janine shuddered. 'I never for one moment thought he was capable of such things. He seemed so nice.'

Marsha checked her watch. If Armstrong had seen the news with his face plastered all over it, he might not turn up today. There was always a chance if he'd got access to a smart phone they didn't know about, but even so.

His father was dying. Often suspects on the run would end up doing something to get themselves caught, thinking they had enough time. Maybe he would want to see Edwin.

'Do you have any contact details for Stephen?' Marsha wanted to know. 'An address or a phone number?'

'I have his mobile.' She handed Marsha a piece of paper. 'Here it is.'

Marsha stepped away for a moment and dialled the number, but it was switched off. She shook her head at Jess.

'Is there anyone else who comes to see him?'

'No, I don't think so.'

'I haven't seen anyone either,' Sadie confirmed.

'May we speak with Edwin? Is he well enough to see us?'

'He won't be able to talk for long. He has lung cancer. It's hard for him.'

'We won't keep him for more than a couple of minutes.'

'No more than that, please.'

Sadie and Janine showed them upstairs to Edwin's room. Edwin was sitting up in bed, his face forlorn as he watched the TV.

'Mr Armstrong?' Marsha held up her warrant card.

Edwin took one look at it, a tear running down his cheek.

'He's in trouble, isn't he?' he said, his breath ragged.

Marsha nodded. 'We believe so. Do you know where we can find him? It's really important, Edwin. We've been to his address, but he wasn't at home.'

Edwin paused. 'St Paul's Church, where some of our family are buried? Solomon's Hollow, perhaps.' He coughed again. 'His sister, Kate's.'

'Where does Kate live?'

'By the cattle market. I... I can't remember.'

'Okay, thank you, Edwin.' Marsha nodded to Janine and Sadie. 'Thank you, too. You've been a great help.'

They went out into the corridor to see Nathan coming towards them. He'd brought two uniformed officers along.

Marsha briefed him on what had been said in Edwin's room. 'Keep a low profile just in case Armstrong appears, but can you arrange for more officers to visit the places he might go, just in case he shows up?'

'Yes, boss, and stay safe!' Nathan shouted after them.

'You see?' Marsha grinned at Jess. 'He loves us really.'

'Yeah, they're not a bad team to work with, I must admit.'

Marsha turned to her, cocked her head. 'You mean you had doubts about us? Pray, no.'

'About me fitting in, perhaps. But never about the team.'

'Good, because I like you, and I'm going to make sure you never leave.'

Marsha's mobile rang, and she answered it. 'Go ahead, Control.'

'I have a Kate Whitcombe, ma'am. She wants to speak to you about her brother, Stephen Armstrong.'

'Put her through.' The line went dead, and then Marsha heard a click. 'Hello, DI Clay speaking. Is that Kate?'

'Yes. I'm calling about my brother. You have a picture of him on the news.'

'We need to speak to him. Do you know where he—'

'It can't be Steve you're after.'

Marsha's shoulders dropped as realisation sank in. 'It's not Stephen, is it?'

'No, it's Robbie. Steve died two days ago.'

CHAPTER FIFTY

'I'm going to find somewhere quiet,' Marsha spoke into her phone. 'Would you speak to me again then? Can you FaceTime?'

Marsha mimed writing to Jess, who handed her a pen. She took down Kate Whitcombe's telephone number and ended the call.

'It isn't Stephen Armstrong,' she said.

'What?' Jess frowned.

'He died on Tuesday. The man we're after, it's his brother, Robbie.'

'Oh no.'

'There's only two years between them, so they must look similar for Tamara to recognise the photo we had of Stephen. Let's go to my car.'

Once they were settled in the front seats, Marsha held the phone up in between them so they could both see the screen. Then she reconnected to Kate via FaceTime.

A woman in her mid-thirties popped up on the screen. She was sitting at a table, a kitchen worktop, units, and a window visible in the background.

The resemblance to the image they had of Stephen was there, and Marsha had no reason to doubt Kate was part of the Armstrong family. She had long, dark hair and a smattering of freckles across her nose. Her eyes were wary, her smile faint. But she was happy to help, which was a bonus right now.

'I'm so sorry to hear about Stephen's death,' Marsha started. 'Can you tell us what happened to him, please?'

'I'm not entirely sure, but from what I've been told, he got drunk at the pub, took a load of sleeping pills and other stuff when he got home, and never woke up,' Kate said. 'He was already drug dependent, so I suppose he felt it was the only way out for him. Although, no one is really sure that he did it intentionally. He perhaps took more of everything than usual, and it proved fatal.'

'Was it you who found him?' Marsha realised how traumatic that would have been if so.

'Yes, I was called by one of his friends. I think Dad has been staying with him, but I haven't managed to catch him there yet, and he doesn't have a mobile phone. He won't have one.' She stopped. 'I'm angry with Steve, to be honest. It seems so selfish, thinking of no one but himself. But then again, I don't blame him. I assume you know our family history.'

'Most of it, I expect, but I'd like to ask you a few more questions. When did you last see Robbie?'

Kate paused for thought. 'A year or so ago. We don't keep in touch anymore. None of us do.'

It struck Marsha then that Kate might not know about Edwin, nor Edwin about Stephen. 'You haven't seen your dad lately?'

'No, not for a while.' Kate's face reddened. 'I bumped into him in town a few months back, but we only spoke for a couple of minutes. He said he was thinking of moving. Our family fell apart when Holly died. She was the baby, a bit of a mistake, Mum used to say.' She smiled fondly. 'When Stephen was sent to prison, things were okay for a while. It was hard for us all to adapt without Holly being there, though. She had always been dancing and singing. She made the house feel alive. So when she died, it was quiet. I missed her so much.

'When Steve came back from juvie, he'd changed. It had really hardened him up. He got it into his head that the accident wasn't his fault, and he said that to Robbie all the time. Robbie was seventeen then. Steve blamed the people who worked at the garage.

'One night, he and Dad had a huge fight, and Steve left. The next we knew he'd been sent to prison for six years for GBH. He beat a young lad to within an inch of his life.

'He served that sentence, came home for a month or so, and then got sent back inside for something similar. It was as if he was on a self-destruct mission. We tried to help him, but he wouldn't listen. I thought his influence hadn't rubbed off on Robbie. I can't believe what he's done. Not this.' Kate placed her head in her hands momentarily.

'It must be hard for you to understand,' Marsha spoke when there was a lull. It was as if Kate needed to talk. 'We can link you up with people to speak to, if you like. You only need to say.'

Kate nodded her thanks.

'What else can you tell me about Robbie?'

'He's divorced with two children. His ex-wife, Tracey, and the kids live in Sandon Street, number six.'

Jess was making notes as she listened to the call.

'Does Robbie know that Stephen has died?' Marsha wanted to know.

'I expect so. Dad will probably have told him.'

'Kate, I know you're not close to your family, and it's not for me to say that you should make amends. But your dad is in Blue Meadows Hospice undergoing palliative care. I'm not sure either of them know about Steve. If you did want to see Edwin, perhaps now would be a good time.'

'Oh.' A tear dripped down Kate's cheek, and she wiped at both eyes, then sniffed. 'Thank you. I'll go and see him.'

'Do you have a recent photo of Robbie you could share with us?'

Kate paused. 'I might have one from a few years ago, but I can't be certain. I'll look, though.'

'Thanks. Can you let me know your address? I'll need to send an officer to talk to you as well.'

Marsha disconnected the call after she had the relevant details, and she and Jess sat in silence for a moment.

'Wow,' Jess said eventually. 'But I'm glad Kate gets to see Edwin now, before he passes.'

'Families are such hard work.' Marsha shook her head. 'I've been extremely lucky with my girls, but I felt for Kate because some of that happened to me, too.'

'Your brother?'

Marsha nodded. 'I know exactly how it feels to have someone taken from your family, to have the heart of it ripped apart. When Joe died, I thought my world had ended. And then the Barker family came after us. They threatened me, my parents, and when they found out I'd joined the police, they came after me again. They wanted to pay me for inside info, but I refused to give it to them. That was a hard year or two as they hounded me. But I'm made of firmer stuff.'

'Do they still bother you?'

Marsha prayed she wouldn't blush as she shook her head. 'Not so much in person, but I hear rumblings every now and then. Dean Barker tends to rear his ugly head every few years. I hate it, but it is what it is. They killed my brother. I will never speak to any of the Barker family unless I have to, never mind get in bed with them, so to speak.'

Jess placed a hand on Marsha's arm. 'I'm so sorry.'

Marsha wiped away a tear that had escaped. 'I know. It upsets me every now and then, particularly in these circumstances. But I will get the whole Barker family one day, bit by bit. Piece by piece. They won't know what's hit them when I do.'

Jess smiled.

'In the meantime, though, we have to alert everyone to the news. With officers stationed at Holly's grave, Kate's and his ex-wife's homes, some at Solomon's Hollow, and more to camp out here, too, unless we get a sighting from the public in between, it's our only hope.'

CHAPTER FIFTY-ONE

Marsha was out of her car now and gathering her team together. Uniformed officers were on their way to the locations mentioned by Edwin Armstrong, plus more were due to arrive here. It was a long shot that Robbie would visit any of them, but it was also all they had at the moment.

The Fiesta wasn't pinging up on any ANPR checks. Armstrong could have swapped the number plates on that vehicle, too, to evade capture.

Until everyone was in place, Nathan was in Edwin's room. Marsha and Jess were going to stay out of view in the rear garden, and Connor the front.

'If you see him coming towards the building,' Marsha told Connor, 'arrest him before he goes inside.'

'I'll sit in my car,' he said. 'I can see the main entrance from there.'

'We don't know if he'll show up, but it's likely to be soon if so. All we can do is cover all entry points. Look out for each other, too.'

'Leave it with us, boss.'

'If we don't pick him up at the places we've thought of,

where else would he go?' Jess asked. 'What about his ex-wife's?'

'It's possible.' Marsha paused. 'I can't help thinking that he'd go to Solomon's Hollow, if anywhere. But then, he's as unpredictable as he's vulnerable.'

She glanced around, wondering which direction, if any, Armstrong would come from. But before she could discuss anything else, Connor spotted something and ran towards the side wall.

'Robbie Armstrong!' he shouted. 'Stop. Police.'

Marsha turned to see Armstrong freeze momentarily and then disappear back over the wall. She and Jess followed after Connor.

'Nathan, he's in the car park!' Marsha used the radio to contact him.

She pressed on, hauling herself up and over the wall and landing on the ground with a squat.

Ahead, she could see Connor and Jess running along the pavement. But then Connor stopped. Seconds later, a red Fiesta came tearing past, Robbie Armstrong the driver.

Marsha went back to the hospice to see Nathan running out of the building.

'He's got away in his car,' she said, getting into her own. 'I'm going after him.'

She drove out of the entrance and waited for Jess who was coming towards her. Marsha reached across and opened the passenger door for her to jump in. Then she sped off after Armstrong.

'We were too far away, boss,' Jess managed to say while she buckled up her seatbelt.

'He can't be far, but we could lose him if we don't spot him straight away.'

At the junction, they looked both ways.

'There!' Jess pointed. Armstrong went left into a side

street a way in the distance. She picked up the radio. 'I'll keep everyone informed.'

The lights and sirens on Marsha's car would alert Armstrong to their presence, but they had to keep the public safe and get them out of the way. She put her foot down and turned left.

'He's gone into Downton Street,' Jess spoke over the airwaves.

Marsha spotted him in front. 'We'll head him off at the far end of the street.'

'I'm right behind you, boss,' Connor informed them.

Marsha checked the rear-view mirror to see him coming up close.

The street was narrow, making it hard to go fast. They weaved in and out of parked cars.

'Why isn't anything coming in the opposite direction when you want it to be?' she shouted in frustration. 'We need to stop him.'

The Fiesta went right with Marsha hot on its tail. It sped blindly over a crossroads, and she pressed her hand on the horn to alert other drivers she was coming through.

A second to slow down to see if it was clear to go, and then she was after him again.

A teenager with a toddler in a pushchair walked along the pavement, her head in a mobile phone. Marsha prayed she didn't veer onto the road without looking. But she didn't even raise her eyes when they sped past.

'Get ready because he'll have to decamp,' she told Jess. 'There's no way out unless he goes on foot across the fields.'

Armstrong lost control on the corner. The car mounted the kerb and went into a hedge.

Marsha pulled up behind him. Jess was already getting out.

Armstrong was off on foot.

'Stop, police!' Marsha shouted, but he ignored her. 'You follow him,' she told Jess. 'I'll head back and cut him off.' Connor was coming up behind her. 'Stay with her, Connor.'

The officers stormed off. Marsha reversed for a few metres and then went left into a side road. With a bit of luck and a tailwind, she might get to Armstrong before he'd be lost in the labyrinth of the housing estate further down.

At the end of the road, she parked and got out. She pounded along the cobblestones of a side entry, finally coming out into the open grassed area.

Armstrong was coming towards her, Jess and Connor chasing behind him.

She raced towards him. He spotted her and veered to the left. Across the other side of the field, Nathan and the uniformed officers were running over.

They were coming at Armstrong on three sides, a triangle chasing him down, closing in step by step. Marsha's lungs wheezed in protest, but still she continued.

One of them had to get to him soon, and she desperately wanted it to be her.

But Jess reached him first. She got a hand to his shoulder. He shrugged her off and continued running. Diving at his ankles, she took him down with her.

Marsha was impressed.

Jess grappled with the suspect. Marsha was the next to get to her. She dropped down on the grass to assist.

In his struggle to get away, Armstrong punched out, hitting Marsha on the cheek. She yelled but didn't stop, straddling his legs while Jess had a knee on his back.

Connor arrived, helping to cuff him.

In between breaths, Jess read him his rights.

'I'm sorry, I'm sorry,' Robbie cried. 'I couldn't help it.'

'Yeah, yeah. That's what they all say.'

Nathan dragged Armstrong to his feet and handed him over to uniform to take back to the station.

'I won't be far behind you,' he told them. 'Just want to make sure everyone is okay here.' He spoke to Jess. 'Nice work,' he complimented.

'Ta very much.' Jess smiled. 'But it was luck that I got to him first.'

'Your first Staffordshire Moorlands collar, though.'

'More paperwork, you mean.' Jess rested her hands on her knees as she caught her breath. 'Are you okay, boss?' she asked Marsha, pointing to the red mark appearing on her cheek.

'Never better.' Marsha grinned, then grimaced at the pain. She put a hand to her face. 'Why am I the only one who got clobbered?'

In the distance, sirens could be heard, signalling the arrival of more police. For now, their job was done.

They had their man.

Now they needed evidence to place him at each scene.

CHAPTER FIFTY-TWO

It was an hour after Marsha had returned to the station when Connor came into the office with his find. He held up an evidence bag.

'This was hidden in the boot of the car,' he said.

Marsha saw a knife, its blade covered in dried blood.

'Gotcha,' she said. 'We should be able to fast-track that.'

Ryan came into the office, a huge smile on his face. 'Well done, Marsha.'

'Thanks, sir. A great team effort, and now for the harder work.'

'Quite a surprise for it to be Robbie, not Stephen Armstrong.'

'It certainly was. Nathan and I have been preparing questions for his interview.'

'Do you think he'll talk?'

'I'm not sure, but I really hope he doesn't go "no comment" to everything. He can't exactly get away with saying not guilty, even if he tries. We have strong evidence now, plus we'll be gathering more over the coming weeks. I just want enough so that the CPS will charge him.'

'I hear he's refused a solicitor.'

'Oh, well, let's go and find out why.'

Robbie Armstrong had been put into interview room three. Marsha and Nathan joined him, set up the recordings and said the necessary before beginning.

'Do you understand everything, Robbie?' Marsha asked.

'Yes.'

'And you're sure you don't want legal representation?'

'No.'

Marsha saw tears in his eyes. She wondered if he was remorseful for what he'd done or panicking now he'd been caught. He faced a long time in prison.

'We're going to ask you some questions now, Robbie. Are you willing to answer them?'

He nodded.

'For the purpose of the recording, can you answer yes for me, please.'

'Yes.'

'Can you tell us where you were and what you did on Monday morning between the hours of eight and nine-thirty?'

Robbie sniffed, then sat forward. 'I ran through every scenario but the one that happened. I would knock on the door. If John Prophet opened it, I was going to shove the blade into his stomach. If it was Sylvia Prophet, I was going to use the knife to lure her into where I could get at John. I didn't want to hurt them both.'

Marsha was shocked at his nonchalance.

'But things never go to plan, do they?' Robbie continued. 'John answered the door, and I stabbed him. Five times. The noise alerted his missus, and she ran at me, screaming out his name. I never meant to hurt her, but to fight her off, I had to backhand her. She went flying into the wall, hitting her head and knocking herself out. Is she okay? I saw she was in hospital.'

'She's stable,' Marsha told him.

Robbie nodded. 'It was then I saw the girls standing in the doorway. I recognised them from photos I'd seen of the family. They were Dan Prophet's kids. I just saw red. I wanted to cause him pain.

'John was falling to the floor by then, and the littlest girl screamed. I hid the knife from view and let him drop slowly to the floor. I told them it was okay, that I'd come to help. I'd seen the man who attacked their nan and granddad, and I needed them to come with me, quickly before he came back.'

Beside Marsha, Nathan cleared his throat. He was obviously as uncomfortable as she was, but they had to listen to his confession.

'The little girl grabbed her big sister's hand, but the older girl was shaking her head. I told her to cover her eyes, that it was okay, but we had to leave. The little girl moved forwards again, and the older one followed her. I told them not to look down and to run to my car outside.'

'That would be the red Fiesta?'

'Yeah. They ran out of the front door, and I put them in the back seat. I asked their names, told them to lie down so no one would see them, and I would take them to the police.' For the first time since the interview began, he started to show some remorse. 'I didn't think it through. I just went into panic mode.'

'You took them to your home, where you held them captive for two nights. Surely you can't panic for so long?' Marsha snapped.

'I wasn't going to hurt them! I never would. But I wanted their mum and dad to suffer like mine had. I wanted them to know what it was like to lose someone you loved. The big one, Tamara, reminded me of Holly.

'I was going to finish what I'd started and then drop them off at the newsagent's, but they kept crying and shouting, and

I thought the neighbours might hear. So I let them go. I watched to make sure they were safe when I dropped them off.'

'That was gallant of you.' Marsha felt Nathan's leg push against hers. She sighed. How was she supposed to keep her cool listening to what he was saying?

'Why Nicholas Adams?' Nathan asked.

'We had a fight in the pub one night. He said some vile things about Steve, and I wasn't having that. Then Steve told me that Nick, Dan, and Chris Osbourne used to play tricks on him all the time. It was just fooling around, they said.' He shook his head. 'They fucking bullied him. I think he was showing off when he was with Holly, and he just lost control. He was quiet until he went to prison. It changed him. *They* changed him.

'He wasn't the brother he'd been before he went inside. He'd learned to stand up for himself. So, when Dad hit out at him, too, Stephen fought back. When he was at home, it was like living in the middle of a boxing ring, on tenterhooks as to which one would start first. I couldn't help him as I wasn't a fighter. I felt such a failure. And then I started drinking, too.

'Eventually, my marriage ended, and I lost the chance to see my kids. They didn't want to know me. I treated their mum so badly.'

'Did you mow Nicholas Adams down in your van?'

He nodded. 'I drove at him with the intention of killing him.'

'I think you need help, Robbie,' Marsha said. 'We can see to it that you get it.'

'Steve was my big brother, and I looked up to him, but he kept on fucking up. You couldn't break the bond between us, until he went to prison because of those – those people.' Robbie was crying openly now. 'I loved my mum, and I hated my dad, yet I wanted him to love me.' He smiled a little then.

'Recently, because he's dying, we started talking. It was nice. So before I left, I had to see him. Can I see him, before he... before...'

'I can't promise, but I'll see what I can do,' Marsha said.

'I'm sorry, I really am. I just couldn't cope with it all. I couldn't see a way out.'

They ended the interview there. They had enough now to charge Robbie while they gathered what they needed over the next few weeks.

Out in the corridor, Marsha blew out a breath. 'That was hard to hear. Are you okay?'

'Yeah, just glad we've got him in custody. You?'

'I'm good. It will hit me later, no doubt.'

'I can't help feeling sorry for him, but it was wrong, what he did. That must have been why he let the girls go.'

'He'll pay the price for that for quite some time. I'm going to tell him about Steve now, so I'll grab an officer who can sit with him afterwards.'

'Want me in with you?'

'No, thanks. I imagine he'll be really upset, and I don't want that to rub off on us both. Still, you know what this means, don't you?'

Nathan grinned. 'Curry?'

Marsha smiled back. 'Curry.'

CHAPTER FIFTY-THREE

Marsha had been downstairs to fetch their takeaway order. Every time they solved a case, they raided their curry fund. They each put twenty pounds into it, and whenever it was running low, topped up again.

'Great result, team,' Marsha said, popping down the bags in the middle of the desks. 'I got you your usual orders, so no squabbling.'

'Thanks, boss.' Emma helped herself to a box with chicken korma written on its lid.

'Yeah, cheers, boss.' Connor dived into the bag nearest to him. 'What a day. I think this will make up for it. My legs are sore from the chase.'

'I guess we'll never know what's going on inside someone's head to make them react like that.' Nathan took the carton Connor handed to him. 'Nice call, boss.'

There was silence in the room for the first few minutes they tucked in, and then the usual ribbing began.

'Are you thinking of staying now that you've worked with us on a case, Jess?' Connor started. 'I mean, now you know that me and Nathan are a pair of arses. Emma will always be a darling, but us?' He ran a finger across his throat. 'We're a bloody nightmare.'

'I wouldn't put it quite so harshly.' Jess laughed. 'I've had worse teams to work with.'

Connor leaned close to Nathan, whispering conspiratorially, 'She doesn't mean that. I think she's a pushover on the quiet.'

'I heard that.'

Connor glanced around, as if trying to locate the source of the gossip.

'Seriously, though, Jess,' Nathan said. 'It's good to have you here. You've fitted in well already.'

'Thanks, Sarge.' Jess beamed.

She didn't see the slight smile that Marsha and Nathan shared.

'Is this a private party or can anyone join in?' Ryan stepped into the room.

'Now that the hard work is over?' Marsha teased, knowing he would find it a joke rather than insubordination. She was proud he gave her free rein for the most part. Ryan was her next-in-command, and she obviously had to check out procedures with him before going off on her own, but he stepped in only when necessary, leaving her and her team to do everything else.

'I got your usual.' Marsha pointed to the bag at the far end of the desks. 'If you eat it now, it should still be warm enough.'

'Thanks, Mum.' Ryan grinned and then looked at everyone. 'And well done, guys. I thought we'd lucked out when the Prophet girls were found safe and well. But you lot really know how to get the job done.'

Nods of appreciation followed, and the conversation turned to more mundane things as they strived to switch off.

Marsha glanced around the room. She had missed Dave

working on this case, with his wit and his input, but Nathan was an excellent replacement, and she was sure Jess would grow in confidence with time.

Connor and Nathan were viewing something on Nathan's phone, giggling like two schoolboys. They caught her looking, and when the screen was turned in her direction, she was surprised to see they were viewing a puppy video on YouTube.

'Aw, you softies,' she said, seeing three Dalmatians race around, tripping over their feet.

'Dogs are far more loyal than humans,' Connor remarked.

'That's very true,' Marsha joined in. 'But I often think Larry is human underneath all that fur.'

'Or a male who uses his charms to get his own way,' Jess added.

'Sexist!' Connor cried as Emma laughed.

'Come to think of it,' Jess nodded fervently, 'yes, it's that.'

Marsha caught Emma's eye and went to perch on the end of her desk.

'What are you smiling about?' she whispered.

'Nothing.' Emma grinned in response.

'I've been watching you, and you can't help yourself. You have a secret!'

'I do.'

Marsha grabbed her hand and took her into the corridor for a moment on their own. 'Spill.'

'Me and Tilly are moving in with Josh.' Josh was one of the traffic cops, based on the first floor. They'd been an item for a year.

Marsha's eyes widened, and she threw her arms around Emma. 'That is such good news. I'm so pleased for you.'

'Thanks. I'm a bit worried about Mum. She isn't used to being on her own, but we won't be far.'

'You have to branch out on your own again sometime. She'll be fine.'

'Do you think? I must admit to feeling really guilty for using her for free child care after school and when I'm doing overtime.'

'I bet she loves it. And you won't be giving that up when you move out, surely?' Marsha shook her head. 'I don't know how I would have coped if Mum didn't live across the road. It's so handy.'

'I'll worry about her, though.'

'And that won't ever stop. Take a chance, Em. Life is too short.' Marsha hugged her again. 'Can I be a bridesmaid at your wedding?'

'That's a bit premature,' Emma exclaimed.

'I want first dibs. I promise to be on my best behaviour.'

'I think you'll find it's a maid of honour.'

'Are you trying to say I'm old?' She stared at her mock sternly. 'Rude.'

Emma chuckled.

Back at their desks, the team were tidying up.

'Right, you lovely lot, time for home. Hopefully, if no one is naughty overnight, we can have a few days catching up with the inevitable mountain of paperwork this case has created.'

There were loud groans from everyone.

'I know, I know, I'm a slave driver. And it's the one thing I hate about this job, but it has to be done. See you all bright and bubbly in the morning.'

There was just Jess left when Marsha switched off her computer and searched her keys out of her handbag.

'That means you, too,' she shouted through to her.

'I'm coming.'

Jess followed her out of the room.

'So, do you fancy having someone to flat-hunt with you

this weekend?' Marsha offered. 'Beats me having to hang around to see Phil's miserable face.'

'I would love that.' Jess held open a door along the corridor for her to walk through. 'I have three to view. You can tell me which ones are best, and which areas, too.'

'Plus I can tell you all the families that you don't want to be living near.'

'That definitely sounds like a plan. I can't wait to have my own front door again.'

'Still not struck on staying at home?'

'I'm fine, but glad it will be temporary. How about you?'

'Well, Phil and I haven't had the talk yet. I assume it will have to happen soon.'

'You have my sympathy, but you'll know what to do when the time is right.'

Marsha nodded. 'Either that or there'll be another murder.'

Jess gasped. 'DI Clay, how can you say that? I don't want to be the one who locks you up.'

'You'd have to catch me first, and I'm way smarter than I look.'

CHAPTER FIFTY-FOUR

Lucy perched on the end of Maisie's bed, watching her daughters. They were sleeping together, something they hadn't done since they were younger.

She didn't want to leave the room, reluctant to let either girl out of her sight, so she stayed still, listening to their breathing.

She had to force herself not to touch them, unable to believe they were home and well.

Earlier, DI Clay had called to tell them the news that Robbie Armstrong would be charged and remanded in custody.

It had been a shock to Dan to discover it wasn't Stephen. He could barely remember his younger brother, Robbie.

The relief had been immense, both she and Dan bursting into tears. There would be time to talk about what had happened tomorrow but, that night, after visiting Sylvia at the hospital, Rachel had left, and they'd ordered pizza, sitting in the garden as a family once more. Both she and Dan had brushed away tears as the girls sat around, sharing and swapping parents to sit with.

Lucy realised how lucky they'd been. Neither she nor Dan had voiced their concerns about not seeing their daughters again. They hadn't wanted to give up the belief that they would come home, unharmed.

But deep down, she *knew* they both thought Tamara and Maisie had been taken for other purposes. She shuddered involuntarily as black thoughts crowded her mind.

How she hated Robbie Armstrong for destroying her family this way.

The light in the hall dimmed, and she turned to see Dan standing in the doorway. Even if Tamara and Maisie didn't want to talk about the past few days, she and Dan needed to. They had to get things sorted, make plans for their future. Decide if they were going to stay together or go their separate ways.

'I'm making coffee,' he whispered so as not to wake the girls.

She stood up and followed him downstairs. Drinks made, they sat in the conservatory, the TV on but neither of them watching.

There was an unease between them that she hated. She might as well say something.

'I'm sorry, Dan,' she said. 'I really—'

'I'm sorry, too.'

His words surprised her. He'd been so angry about the affair, and now — now their girls were back, had it changed him? It had certainly changed her.

'But why Chris?'

Lucy's heart sank. She didn't want to talk about the finer details, knowing they would hurt him. But she'd set out to be truthful, so she braced herself.

'He was there when you weren't.'

Dan blew out air, deflated by her words.

'I won't say it just happened because it didn't. I knew

what I was doing. But I felt lonely, Dan. You were leaving at six and not coming home until after nine most evenings. Even Saturday afternoons and weekends were taken up with paperwork. I was... lost without you, but I didn't know how to tell you. Chris was just there. It was only a few times. We didn't meet regularly. I'm so sorry, still.'

'Do you love him?'

'No I don't.' She shook her head. 'I felt so guilty whenever I came home afterwards. Dirty, sneaky, disgusted with my actions. Not good enough to be with you.'

Dan sat quiet for a moment. 'It hurts, Lucy. It really hurts that you'd do that to me.'

'I know.'

'When Dad retired, he told everyone, including you, that he signed the business over to me. He didn't. He said I had to prove I was worthy of it, that I could do it myself and not cock up, for twelve months.'

'Oh, Dan, why didn't you tell me?'

'Because I was embarrassed. That twelve months turned into nearly two years, and I still don't have full control. It played on my mind that he was right about me being useless.'

'But that's not true.'

'I couldn't do what he did by myself, I struggled. And the more I tried, the more I had to be at work. The hours away from you and the girls weren't me not wanting to come home, not wanting to be with you. I was...' He ran a hand through his hair. 'I was drowning in paperwork. Being a mechanic is nothing compared to running the whole show. Dad seemed to do everything with ease.'

'John got everyone else doing the work! That's what the staff are paid for.'

'I wasn't man enough to ask for help. People were relying on me, and I didn't want Dad to find out he was right.'

'No, he was wrong.' Lucy moved to sit next to Dan. She

dared to cover his hand with hers. 'You had a go, and it didn't work out as you'd hoped. But that's not the end of the world, and it's braver of you to continue working at it than for your father to punish you just because he could. I don't know why John was such a bully, but I'm glad I don't see that in you.'

Dan gave a faint smile.

'And this is something that can easily be rectified, even if your mum wants to keep everything in her name. *You* are the business now, and she knows that. She's always going on about how proud she is of you.'

'She was always ridiculed by him whenever she mentioned it.'

'But she never stopped saying it, regardless. She thinks the world of you, Dan, and so do the staff. You have a great team there. You only have to explain to them, and they'll be there for you, especially after what's happened.' She paused, took a deep breath. 'I can help, too, if you'll let me. I can do extra hours. I'd like that. I can take on more responsibility for things. We can work together as a team.'

'What about Chris? I can't work with him there. Not after...' His voice cracked. 'I just can't.'

'I thought you told him to leave.' She smiled shyly.

'He won't just up and go.'

'I don't think he'll want to stay now that it's all out in the open.'

'I hate that everyone knows.'

'Maybe that will make him feel too uncomfortable.'

Dan looked at the floor then. '*I* feel weak having you back, knowing that you've slept with that... that double-crossing bastard, but I love you, Lucy. I miss what we used to be, and I don't want life to be like this.'

Lucy smiled at him tentatively. Was he giving her a second chance? She didn't deserve one but, if so, she wasn't going to muck it up.

Tears pricked her eyes. She realised how much she wanted to kiss him, start the passion all over again. She wanted those hands to take her to higher heights, those fingers to run through her hair.

He glanced at her then. 'Can you give me time?'

Lucy nodded. 'However much you need.'

CHAPTER FIFTY-FIVE

'Hi, Mum, it's only me,' Jess shouted through as she opened the front door.

Pam came rushing from the living room, her face a little flushed. 'There you are, love. I've been waiting for you.'

'We ordered in curry, and—'

'Well, when I say *I've* been waiting for you, I meant to say we.'

'We?' Jess frowned and followed Pam into the living room.

Reece Masters was sitting on the settee.

Jess went cold, and, for a moment, she thought she might faint. How could he be here, inside the house?

He looked fresh in jeans and a white designer T-shirt, and he'd had his hair cut shorter than she remembered. But his eyes were dark, and there was no emotion behind his smile.

It was what he was like, Jekyll and Hyde. He could fool the best of people that he was a nice person. Like he'd done to Pam, no doubt.

But only she knew the real man behind the smokescreen.

'What are you doing here?' Jess asked, unable to keep the

distress from her voice. It wasn't her mum's fault that he'd charmed his way in.

'I was in the area, and thought I'd pop in to see how you are.'

'I'm fine.'

'So I hear. Congratulations on solving your first case in your new team. I bet you're so proud of your little girl, Pam.'

'Oh, yes, I am.' Pam nodded fervently. 'We were just watching it on the news, weren't we, Reece?'

'We were.'

His smile was sickly. Jess wished she was brave enough to reach over and swipe it off his face. How dare he pretend everything was okay between them.

She'd been wrong not to tell Pam about him, but she hadn't wanted to worry her. There was no way she'd anticipated this kind of trickery, and she certainly didn't think Reece would wheedle his way in here to get nearer to her.

Once he'd gone, she'd have to tell her everything.

'Would you like a cuppa?' Pam asked.

'No, thanks. But seeing as you've come so far, Reece, perhaps you'd like to go out for a drink? The village pub is only a few minutes away.'

'I think that's a great idea.' Reece stood up and turned to Pam. 'Thank you so much for your hospitality. It's been a pleasure to meet you. I can tell you Jess is a force to be reckoned with at work, and I – we – miss her already.'

Pam tittered.

Jess rolled her eyes discreetly. 'I won't be long, Mum.'

'You take your time and enjoy yourself!'

Jess closed the door and walked along the path to where Reece was waiting for her on the pavement. As soon as she knew she was out of hearing range, she laid into him.

'What the hell do you think you're playing at? You have no right to visit my mum.'

'I didn't. I came to see you.'

'So you thought you'd get her on side? Let her think you're a wonderful person so she doesn't believe me when I say that I hate you?'

'Surely not.' Reece sighed, as if he was chastising a tearaway toddler. 'I know we'll patch things up eventually.'

'We'll do nothing of the sort.'

He reached for her hand and marched off with her.

'Let go of me.' She pulled away, but he kept a firm grip, pinching her fingers.

When they got to the end of the pavement and turned the corner, he pushed her up against the wall of the last house.

Out of sight, there was no one to see. He came closer, covering her body with his own.

'God, I've missed you.' He sniffed close to her neck. 'The scent of you. The feel of you.'

'Get your hands off me.'

'Don't be like that. I could take you, right here, if you like?'

Jess stayed calm, quiet on the outside. She had to let him think he was in control until she could get away. But when he dropped his lips close to hers, she moved her head.

She would not allow him to do that.

He grabbed her chin, squeezing it crudely. 'Don't mess me about, Jess. If it's a bit of rough you need, then I can oblige.'

He leaned in again to kiss her and, when his head came closer, she bit his bottom lip. Hard.

The look in his eyes was comical. She took the opportunity to draw back her leg and kneed him in the groin.

He dropped to the ground in agony.

She grabbed him by the hair. Even though she was terrified of what he'd do to her later, she had to show him she wasn't afraid.

'Come near me again,' she bent over to speak to him, 'and I'll get a restraining order on you, do you hear me?'

Reece groaned.

'Do you fucking hear me?' she shouted.

'Yes!'

'Good.' She stood up, shoulders held high. She wasn't a violent person, nor did she curse a lot, but she was certain when she'd calmed down, she'd be glad of what she'd done.

For now, she had got away with it. It wouldn't be the last time he came creeping around, so she didn't want to antagonise him too much. He would still come after her.

Because he was a stupid bastard who wouldn't take no for an answer.

But she would do what she'd said.

First thing tomorrow, she would file for a restraining order. She wouldn't wait. If he didn't leave her alone, she would have him arrested.

'You won't get away with this,' he said, sitting now as he caught his breath. 'I'll keep coming back, and each time you reject me, I'll make you pay in some other way.'

'Grow up and get a life,' she muttered and walked away.

She half expected him to come racing after her, then drag her to the floor and assault her. But she kept on going.

When she got to his car, she took a photo of it. She'd hate doing all that again, recording evidence and noting down everything he did or said. But she would do it. It was her right to feel safe.

It was always her right.

CHAPTER FIFTY-SIX

Marsha let herself in the house and was greeted by Larry who almost tripped up in his haste to get to her.

'Hello, hello,' she laughed. 'I see someone is happy to see me.'

She hung her bag over the bannister and stopped. There were two suitcases at the bottom of the stairs.

A rush of dread shot through her.

She went into the kitchen to find it empty, and then through to the living room. Phil was sitting upright on the edge of the settee, looking apprehensive.

'What's going on?' she asked, her voice quiet.

'I see you got your man, congratulations. I'm proud of you.' He paused, spotting the bruising on her cheek. 'What happened to your face? Are you okay?'

'Occupational hazard. I got in the way of a fist when we arrested him. Can you remember Stephen Armstrong from school?'

'Did he kill his sister in a car accident?'

'That's the one.'

'I haven't seen him in a while, why do you ask?'

'It was his brother, Robbie, who we arrested. Stephen died of an overdose.'

'Robbie? He was younger than Steve, wasn't he?'

'Yes, a couple of years.'

'Did he say why?'

'He did, but you know I can't tell you that. I expect the media will be full of speculation, though.'

'Wow. Never a dull moment when you're around.'

His smile was faint, but Marsha knew what he meant.

'I'm fine, though, thanks.' She pointed to her face. 'It's just a bruise.'

Silence fell on the room. Marsha didn't want to fill it. Eventually, Phil started to talk.

'I've wanted to speak to you for a while, but I don't think—'

'You're leaving?'

He nodded.

'It's not that I don't want to discuss things.' Marsha sat down across from him. Already, they seemed like strangers. 'I suppose I didn't want it to get to this stage if we did.'

'I get that. I've been trying to find the right words for a few weeks now.'

'Is it really so serious that we can't work things out?'

She hadn't expected to say that.

'Do you want to?' Phil replied.

Did she want to?

'I don't know.' She felt it best to be truthful. It wouldn't be fair on either of them, or the girls, to continue something that was broken beyond repair.

But then he dropped his bombshell.

'I... I've met someone else.'

She looked up sharply, gasping at the hurt she felt with such few words.

'Oh,' was all she managed to say. Because even though she

might not want to be with Phil anymore, it stung to know that she'd already been replaced. He hadn't even gone, and he was shagging someone else.

'Do I know her?' she queried, gnawing at her bottom lip.

He shook his head. 'It's someone from work.'

'Now, there's a surprise,' she muttered. 'And there was you always going on at me that there were affairs throughout the police force. Hypocrite.'

'It wasn't like that. We just... we.'

'Spare me the details. I have a vivid imagination.' She gave a weak smile then. 'I don't want our marriage to end, but I know it's over. Well, obviously, it's over for you more than it was for me.'

'I tried to talk to you!'

His tone was accusatory, but Marsha ignored him. She didn't want to know, but she had to. Call it torture, but she had to find out.

'How long have you been seeing her?' She wondered how this conversation would have played out with Dan and Lucy Prophet after the news of Lucy's affair with Chris Osbourne. Nathan and Amy, too. She could certainly empathise with Dan and Amy's pain.

'A few months.' He hung his head.

'Right.' Tears stung the backs of her eyes, but it was because she was feeling sorry for herself more than the thought of him leaving.

'Does she have her own place?'

Phil nodded. 'I'm moving in with her.'

'Tonight?'

'Yes, she's waiting for me.'

'And what about us? The house, the girls? I won't include Larry as he's staying put.'

Phil stroked the dog's head, curled up beside him without a care in the world. 'I'm going to miss him. And the girls. But we can't live like this, Marsha. It's not fair on any of us.'

'And the house?' she repeated.

'Let's just see how things go, but I won't be putting you out on the street, if that's what you mean.'

'That's very good of you.' Her voice dripped with sarcasm.

Phil stood up. 'I'd best be on my way.'

'Bye then.'

She stayed seated while he left the room, loaded his cases into the car, and reversed out of the drive.

Now, Larry's snores were the only thing she could hear.

Marsha sighed into the empty room. 'Well, that's that, then.'

She realised it hadn't hurt as much as she'd thought.

Sure, there would be tantrums and arguments over things in the future, and she'd have to tell the girls in the morning, but a calm had washed over her.

There could be no more second-guessing, no more wondering "what if he left?".

Phil had gone. Her marriage was over.

And Marsha was still standing.

***

First of all, I'd like to say a huge thank you for choosing to read Missing Girls. I hope you enjoyed my first outing with Marsha Clay and her team.

For all the readers from Leek and the surrounding Staffordshire Moorlands, I hope you don't mind me taking liberties with the place you live. Creating a police station for example, streets and areas for crimes to take place among real ones, are the only way I can think of to not offend anyone.

If you did enjoy Missing Girls, I would be grateful if you would leave a small review or a star rating on your Kindle. I'd love to hear what you think. It's always good to hear from you.

***

Before you go, would you like to join my reader group? I love to keep in touch with my readers, and send a newsletter every few weeks. I also reveal covers, titles and blurbs exclusively to you first, and give away prizes.

Join Team Sherratt

ALL BOOKS BY MEL SHERRATT

These books are continually added to so please
Click here for details about all my books on one page

Detective Allie Shenton (complete 6 book series)

Taunting the Dead

Follow the Leader

Only the Brave

Broken Promises

Hidden Secrets

Twisted Lives

The Estate Series

Somewhere to Hide

Behind a Closed Door

Fighting for Survival

Written in the Scars

Don't Look Behind You

DS Grace Allendale Series (complete 4 book series)

Hush Hush

Tick Tock

Liar Liar

Good Girl

Standalone Psychological Thrillers

Watching over You

The Lies You Tell

Ten Days

The Life She Wants

ACKNOWLEDGMENTS

Thanks, as always, to my amazing fella, Chris, who looks out for me so that I can do the writing. I wish I could take credit for all the twists in my books but he's actually more devious than I am when it comes down to it – in the nicest possible way. We're a great team – a perfect combination.

Thanks to Alison Niebieszczanski, Caroline Mitchell, Louise Ross, Imogen Clark, Sharon Sant and Talli Roland, who give me far more friendship, support and encouragement than I deserve.

Finally, thank you to Team Sherratt, and all my readers who keep in touch with me via Twitter and Facebook. Your kind words always make me smile – and get out my laptop. Long may it continue.

ABOUT THE AUTHOR

Ever since I can remember, I've been a meddler of words. Born and raised in Stoke-on-Trent, Staffordshire, I used the city as a backdrop for my first novel, TAUNTING THE DEAD, and it went on to be a Kindle #1 bestseller. I couldn't believe my eyes when it became the number 8 UK Kindle KDP bestselling books of 2012.

Since then, I've sold over two million books. My writing has come under a few different headings - grit-lit, thriller, whydunnit, police procedural, emotional thriller to name a few. I like writing about fear and emotion – the cause and effect of crime – what makes a character do something.

But I'm a romantic at heart and have always wanted to write about characters that are not necessarily involved in the darker side of life. Coffee, cakes and friends are three of my favourite things, hence I write women's fiction under the pen name of Marcie Steele.

All characters and events featured in this publication, other than those clearly in the public domain, are entirely fictitious and any resemblance to any person, organisation, place or thing living or dead, or event or place, is purely coincidental and completely unintentional.

All rights reserved in all media. No part of this book may be reproduced in any form other than that which it was purchased and without the written permission of the author. This e-book is licensed for your personal enjoyment only. No part of this text may be reproduced, transmitted, downloaded, decompiled, reverse engineered, or stored in or introduced into any information storage and retrieval system, in any form or by any means, whether electronic or mechanical, now known or hereinafter invented, without the express written permission of the author.

Missing Girls © Mel Sherratt
E-edition published worldwide 2023
Kindle edition Copyright 2023 © Mel Sherratt